AN ELDERBERRY FALL

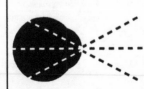

This Large Print Book carries the
Seal of Approval of N.A.V.H.

AN ELDERBERRY FALL

RUTH P. WATSON

THORNDIKE PRESS
A part of Gale, a Cengage Company

Farmington Hills, Mich • San Francisco • New York • Waterville, Maine
Meriden, Conn • Mason, Ohio • Chicago

LIBRARY OF CONGRESS CIP DATA ON FILE.
CATALOGUING IN PUBLICATION FOR THIS BOOK
IS AVAILABLE FROM THE LIBRARY OF CONGRESS

ISBN-13: 978-1-4328-5435-5 (hardcover)

Published in 2018 by arrangement with Strebor Books, an imprint of Atria Books, a division of Simon & Schuster, Inc.

Printed in Mexico
1 2 3 4 5 6 7 22 21 20 19 18

Dear Reader:

We first introduced Ruth P. Watson with her debut novel, *Blackberry Days of Summer,* which conjures up images of *The Color Purple.* Now she returns with her poignant sequel, *An Elderberry Fall,* historical fiction set in the 1920s.

Carrie Parker, newly married to Simon, has moved to Richmond, Virginia, in contrast to her rural roots of Jefferson County. There she experiences motherhood with her son, Robert, while pursuing her dreams of becoming a teacher. Simon travels throughout the country playing baseball on colored teams aspiring to climb the ranks in the beloved sport. Carrie also finds her flirtatious neighbor, Nadine, a challenge as she adjusts to city life.

Mystery continues to surround the murder of Herman Camm, her stepfather, in this whodunit. Then suspense arises again when Willie, the husband of popular nightclub singer, Ms. Pearl, is shot and killed.

The novel is a tale of discovery, doubt and deceit written with the flavor of a bygone era. Follow the appealing cast of characters, and if you haven't read *Blackberry Days of Summer,* find out how it all starts.

Thanks also for supporting the authors under Strebor Books. We truly appreciate the love. For more information on our titles, please visit simonandschuster.com.

Blessings,
Zane
Publisher
Strebor Books
www.simonandschuster.com

This novel is dedicated to the dreamers.
It can be done.
Stay faithful, my friends!

ACKNOWLEDGMENTS

"To God be the glory for the things he has done."

To all of my ancestors who've paved the way for me to live free, I thank you.

To the readers who purchased *Blackberry Days of Summer* and enjoyed it enough to request another book, I thank you.

To my future readers, I thank you.

My family and friends mean the world to me. I thank you for the love and support. And, to the book clubs and readers who were curious enough to crack open my book, your support is reason to keep writing.

Relax now and enjoy *An Elderberry Fall.*

PROLOGUE

"A Colored Man Found Dead" was written in tall letters on the front page of the Clinch Valley newspaper. *The Richmond Planet* also mentioned the murder. "His frostbitten purple lips kissed the cold ground while the frigid wind whistled a solemn lullaby through the barren trees."

In the article about his murder, the condition of the body was described in vivid detail. "Sticky blood splattered all around his lifeless body. His dark beady eyes were wide open and staring straight ahead. The undertaker put a copper penny over his eyelids to keep them closed."

The news had the entire damn community reacting. The Baptist preacher was especially concerned; another soul had gone before he could lay hands on him and make the call to the Almighty to save his sinning soul. The rumors had been spawned. It had ignited a sick excitement of concern about Herman

Camm's earthly departure. Everybody was talking. But, I didn't utter a word. I'd learned how to bury my feelings. The news of his death brought with it a certain air of peace, and for the first time in over a year, I felt relieved in the midst of confusion. As a wave of fear replaced the rattled nerves of the small farm community, the men folks checked their guns for ammunition, and others polished and sharpened their weapons. As they searched their minds for whomever his killer could be, they rolled their eyes and gazed at each other, afraid they might be in the company of a real criminal. There was no pity in my heart for Herman Camm. I was somewhat relieved, even glad, but not gloating. Cheering was a sin. It was definitely my signal to leave town. Simon's letter arrived right on time.

"This is for you," Momma said, and handed me the letter, folded, as if she was trying to hide it. I had been praying for a way out and when I read his note, I cried for joy, borrowed a suitcase from Aunt Ginny and headed to the train station.

CHAPTER 1

On February 4th, 1921, I gulped a breath of fresh air before I took the last step down the train steps onto solid ground. The brisk wind caressed my skin, and alerted me to a new reality. "So this is Richmond, Virginia," I said to myself, gazing around at the cobblestone sidewalks and cars. My six-month-old son, Robert, had his head resting on my shoulder as I struggled with my overloaded suitcase, straining every muscle in my body, but I could not have cared less. Who would have believed a young girl like me would be here — in the big city, with streetcars and tall buildings and with colored people strutting around in fine, fashionable outfits, like the kind white folk wore in Jefferson County on special occasions? The coloreds appeared proud, like they owned the town. It felt good, and I fought to slow my heart down from the rush of anxiety. It was certainly different here. Most of the folks I knew probably thought I would live forever in Jefferson County amongst the sour memories and shame from the child I bore out of wedlock. But I was not so ready to stay there. When Simon asked me to come to Richmond, Virginia, my real transformation began.

My child, Robert, is beautiful. He is almost flawless. Each day I study the ridges around his little fingers, waiting to see if his tan color and fine features and that innocent, charismatic smile will remain. He favors me for the most part. However, there are times when his eyes seem dark and mysterious, and it sends chills throughout my body.

Robert, Simon and I live in a small apartment on the west side of Richmond — Jackson Heights, they call it. It's the colored section of town. It is a fine neighborhood, with shrubbery and flowers planted tastefully in front of well kept tenement houses and single-family row homes. Our place is a small, brick, two-story house with a cast-iron fence around it. Alongside the yard is an elderberry bush, which reminds me of the sweet jam Momma made in the fall. Most of the neighborhood residents are colored and oblivious to the surrounding communities. Everything seems to be within walking distance — the grocer, tailor, the cobbler, and the feed and seed store. The corner store has everything we need. Farmers are unloading crates of vegetables every day, and hanging inside are hams, and there is a meat counter where slices of select meat can be packaged. It is well stocked, and I am overwhelmed that I no longer have to work in a field with the hot sun beaming down on me. Simon has a rooster and two hens in the backyard, mainly for eggs. But, I can imagine them on the table stuffed with cornbread dressing.

We share our backyard with a couple downstairs. They are on the front porch every day sitting in a porch swing with wide smiles swept across their faces as if the stresses of life had floated past them even though they are different from others in the neighborhood. Most people stare transfixed by their difference. The lady is white, very pale, and the man is colored. Most feel their living together is a disgrace to everyone around them. It is alright with me because they seem happy. And from where I come from, happiness is the center of life and satisfaction. The man is tall and very dark, almost as dark as a midnight sky. He is clean, somewhat handsome and solid in build. She is a petite lady of normal height, a brunette, with barely any frown lines or wrinkles and sky-blue eyes. The Halls are at least sixty years old, but they don't look it. Directly across the street from us is another strange, but beautiful couple. The man is rugged in appearance like most railroad workers. He has long lashes like those of a woman, thick bushy hair and flawless caramel skin. Though handsome, he is never well-groomed. His wife is also attractive. She is dark chocolate with a lot of hair that falls to her shoulders, and bounces as she walks; her pouty lips are the kind the old people swear are sexy. Those neighbors have two children. Simon and I are getting used to the newness of city life, the sounds of the streetcars, the pinging of the church clock, and the whispers of voices walking down the street. On steamy summer nights, the neighborhood seems to explode. Vague voices and outbursts of laughter are heard from blocks away. It's a jovial place. The sounds of crickets chirping are drowned out by the hissing of the steam shooting out of the trains and streetcars starting and stopping along its route through town. The action is hypnotic. I find myself loathing going to sleep, because I relish the sounds of city life so much. It is invigorating.

I can't help wondering about Momma and

her life in a world shadowed with trees. She is alone now, with painful memories about a time all of us would love to forget. But, somehow the past always come back to you in some form. Carl, my brother, is still in Jefferson County, and yards away from my mother. He is just like my papa, strong-willed and no-nonsense. He is the strength she needs right now. When Camm was murdered, I'd waited for her to lose it all — break down in tears — but instead her face appeared less tense, relaxed. Just like for me, a burden had been lifted from my mother's shoulders.

Simon is all I need right now. He is such a handsome man, physically and mentally strong. He is truly mine in every form, something I never thought would happen; and I adore ever inch of his being. I quiver sometimes just thinking about how complete he makes me feel. "Oh, Lawd, is this right?" I say to myself, and feel warm chills travel over my skin. He says he loves me, and acts like it, too. He is so attentive to me and Robert. Along with most women we are around, the lady across the street is always staring at my husband. I smile shyly at her, knowing she'd better stay in her place, because he has chosen me.

CHAPTER 2

"You ought to leave that precious little boy right here with me," Mrs. Hall said to me, with a proper Northern accent, early one morning as she sat on her front porch. I was on my way to the corner store. Robert was straddling my hip with his bottle in his hand and his head heavy on my shoulder. He was attached to his bottle. I had tried breastfeeding him, but my nipples became sore and blistered. My Aunt Ginny told me to rub some camphor on them, but I hated it and the bottle was convenient, except for the cost of the cow's milk.

"Mrs. Hall, he is always on the go. I don't want to burden you with a baby."

She stared at me, puzzled, "What are neighbors for, then?" I liked what she said, so I smiled. She fixated her sky-blue eyes on Robert, and he lifted his head and smiled cheerfully.

Her husband, who was rocking in the

chair beside her, egged her on without hesitation. "That's right" he mumbled, "we don't mind; we love children."

Robert is a thick child, unlike his father, who was puny compared to my Simon, who is athletically built and over six feet tall. Robert's hands are chunky and his arms thick, with folds on them. His teeth are coming in and he is gumming on his fists and everything else he can put into his mouth. He is a heavy child, and full of energy, bouncing around in my arms without a care. His jovial little smile can charm the best of them. Every time I take him out, women are often complimenting him on his beauty, and in return, a smile spreads across his chunky little face.

Before I could answer, Mrs. Hall reached out for Robert, who, without hesitation, threw up his tiny arms for her to take him. She pulled him out of my arms and Robert stared into her eyes as if he was hypnotized. And afterward, he snuggled his head into her breast. I never thought he would take to someone so easily, but he liked her from the moment we met them. I stood waiting for my child to come back into my arms, but he appeared comfortable in Mrs. Hall's pale, thin arms. I felt relief when she held Robert. Dragging him with me wherever I went was wearing me and him out. Simon rushing off again to play with the Negro League had me perplexed. The assumption that it was okay bothered me. What could I say? I needed him more than ever. As I walked the three blocks down the street, I couldn't help but wonder about my life. Teaching was the only current running through my head, and that was the only thing I intended on doing.

The walk to the corner was what I needed, the air still and sweet with the scent of fading honeysuckle and lilacs. The morning sunlight hovered above my head, filling me with warmth. The street was empty and quiet. As I passed one house, the aroma of fatback seeped into the streets. However, I was the only person walking down the street so early in the morning. I had remained loyal to Mama's efforts to get up early. "Peoples get more done in the mo'ning," she'd say. The merchant on the corner was also a daybreak riser; he opened his doors every morning at seven on the dot. He was a short, bald, colored man, who always wore a butcher's apron. He greeted me as soon as I stepped in the door.

"Good morning, young lady. I see you know the early bird catches the worm." It was a phrase I'd heard him say every time I came before the normal crowd. I wasn't sure if I was getting any special care, but I knew the produce was always fresh.

"Yes, sir, "I answered.

"What can I get for you?" He was always pleasant, and treated everyone well. Already shopping was the couple across the street, Nadine and Jessie, holding a package of wrapped cheese with *5 cents* written on it. Their children probably were still snuggled under their bedcovers, unlike my Robert who woke up with the sun. As I thought about him, I hoped he was not giving Mrs. Hall too much trouble. The store was well stocked. It had everything from eggs to hams, and in the very back of the store were a washing machine, tin tubs, and two pot-belly cast-iron stoves. On my shopping list was butter, cheese, souse meat, coffee and saltine crackers. I don't have to worry about milk as the milkman delivers milk twice a week.

I gathered my things and handed the merchant two dollars to pay. He nodded to say it was right, and then I picked up my merchandise and headed through the door. I walked briskly back to the apartment house, right past two ladies chatting in the middle of the cobblestone sidewalk, without speaking to them, concerned my baby was in need of me. When I got to the porch, Robert was lying on Mrs. Hall's petite chest. He saw me and smiled. "He was no trouble at all. We never had children and it was a delight looking after him. I know you are alone most of the time, so if you need some help with him, let us know," Mrs. Hall said, patting Robert on the back.

"Yes, Ma'am," I answered and waited for Robert to acknowledge my opened arms and reach for me. I thanked them and took him up the steps to our apartment. Mr. Hall grabbed my groceries from the steps and followed me up the stairs to my apartment. "Thank you, Mr. Hall," I said and he put the items on the table and left.

It was Friday. The weekend was about to begin, and I couldn't wait for the man I married to return home. The Colored League was busy these days, and Simon was gone most weekends. Within six months, Simon had bounced from team to team. He spent a month with the Washington Patriots, and now he was playing with an independent team over in the Blue Ridge Mountains. He was yearning for the opportunity to play against Pete Hill, of the Detroit Stars, who hit more runs last year than Babe Ruth, because the colored boys play longer games. He loved living out of a suitcase. He usually came home during the week, but the team gave them a weekend a month to spend with the family.

We got married the first week I arrived in Richmond. On Wednesday while the sun was high we went to the courthouse and got a marriage license and the gospel preacher around the corner scolded us about love and then married us in his parlor — his wife the witness. "Marriage ain't no game. It is real and serious. Y'all need to know this before I marry y'all," he said.

"We understand, Reverend," Simon answered and I nodded. I had on the same mundane tan dress I'd worn to church many times before. The only special thing about our wedding was our love. One day we plan on doing it the right way, in front of all the people we admire and respect. I plan on wearing a gown, too — a white one. White is for anybody who wears it, Ginny told me. But, most folks in Jefferson County had memories like elephants. They felt virgins were only entitled to white. I knew better, since they all had skeletons in their closets, and nobody had enough white to cover those skeletons up.

The clock on the kitchen wall read six o'clock. I had glanced at it so many times; the time seemed to stand still. Simon should be walking in the door at any time, I thought, turning over the salt fish frying in the cast-iron frying pan. Simon loves salted fish, and I had soaked it all night, making sure everything was ready for his homecoming. The aroma was irritating. I cracked open the kitchen window, so the fumes and scent would escape before sticking to my clothes. The fried apples and potatoes were already done and warming in the oven. And Robert was scooting around on the floor, his bright eyes wide open, smiling as if he knew Daddy was on his way. The apartment was clean. I had scrubbed the floors that afternoon and finished folding the clothes. Everything was in place. The ice-cold lemonade was in the ice box, and the pudding cake I'd baked early that morning was ready for dessert.

A frown of worry rippled across my face at the mere thought of Simon traveling with the baseball league. I worried about where he would eat and lay down his head at night. Colored boys had to stay in the homes of the volunteers in the community. I worried because the white man was mighty bitter about the Emancipation Proclamation and would forever hold a grudge. We just wanted what they enjoyed, acceptance.

Robert was now sitting on the floor waving his little arms for me to pick him up. He was such a happy little child and I hoped that never changed. I bent down to pick him up just as the front door sprang wide open. "I made it," Simon said, smiling from ear to ear.

Robert heard his daddy's voice and almost jumped out of my arms toward Simon.

"Hi, Honey. We have been waiting all day for you to get home," I said, grinning from ear to ear.

"I know you have," he said, as he put his arms around me and little Robert, squeezing us so close we could feel each other's heart beat.

Simon is gorgeous and tall, a muscular man with beautiful, almond-shaped eyes that compel you to stare and gaze directly into them as if they are magnets. I can't help staring, not because I want to, but because I'm compelled to each and every time I see him.

"Baby, I am so happy to get a few days rest," he commented. As he held me and Robert close, I had to fight back the chill that was overtaking my body. Simon took Robert out of my arms and swung him up in the air. I removed the last piece of fish from the grease, and dropped a few hush-puppies in the oil.

Simon took his duffle bag along with Robert in his arms and went into the bedroom. Robert gazed at Simon in total admiration; and from the smile on Simon's face, he enjoyed it. I put two pieces of fish, apples and potatoes on a plate for Simon and made one for me. I poured us a glass of lemonade. We sat down for dinner only after Simon pulled me in close and kissed me deeply, pushing his tongue into my mouth, and my body quivered.

Our kitchen table seats four. However, we never have had visitors, except on the one occasion when Momma took the train here for a visit. It is a cozy little space, just enough for a small family. When we are together at the table, it is a reminder of the times when I lived in Jefferson County and Papa was living. We ate together and Papa made us children feel like our day was special, even when it was spent working out in the sun all day. Now Simon always had a story to tell, and most times they made me laugh so hard I would cry.

"Carrie, I'll be home for exactly five days this time, so don't try to fatten me up, and make me lose my job," Simon said, right after finishing the last bit of lemonade in his glass. Robert was still slobbering food down his cheeks. Simon mashed his apples and potatoes with a fork and fed him.

"I'm not fattening you up. I don't want you too thin."

"Well, I've got to stay fit, so I can play ball. One day we are going to be in the big league, girl," he said, smiling cunningly at me.

I smiled. The big league sounded promising, and even rewarding, but my husband being away was not the kind of marriage I had prayed for. "Yeah, I know."

Robert was full and now his eyes were heavy as his little head rested on his daddy's broad chest. I took him out of Simon's arms, undressed him and laid him in his bed. His little body, totally limp, was fast asleep. Tonight he would be going to bed without a bath. The selfish me couldn't wake him up, because I wanted all of Simon's attention tonight. After watching Robert's little chest heave up and down, I went back into the kitchen.

"Simon, I wish you could stay longer. Robert is growing up so fast. Did you see his new tooth coming in?"

I sat down in Simon's lap. "Yes, I did. What I am doing, Carrie, is for our family. I want to be here for every change he experiences."

His eyes were like magnets, and as I stared

into them, I could feel as if I was him, and shared his passion for baseball, and family. "I miss you, and I don't know that many people."

"You know the Halls, and Nadine and Jessie, and Hester. The people around here are nice and they will look out for you. I don't have to worry when I'm gone."

Everything he was saying was true, but it did nothing for my yearning inside for him to be home all the time. Having Simon around all the time was something I wanted more than anything. He was everything I could ever hope for in a man.

He had stayed home for the first two months when I arrived in Richmond. He wouldn't leave my side, especially after our first nights together. It took him weeks of assurance before I could be a real wife to him. He would hold me in his arms, and let me cry out all the bitterness I had held captive in my head. Things like the day Momma made me stay home while she went to work for Mrs. Ferguson, and Herman Camm penned me in my room and took full advantage of my body and my thoughts. Carrying Robert for all those months was the worst feeling I'd ever experienced, so making love to my husband was the last thing on my mind.

We made it through it all one night when the weather was brisk, the moon was bright, and a late summer breeze was whirling against the window pane, yet it was hot inside. I had just put Robert in his crib, and he was sound asleep with his thumb in his mouth. So comfortable, he'd sleep the entire night. Simon started like he always did. He'd kiss me on the forehead, since I was so much shorter than him, and then kiss me all over my face. I could feel him. When my breathing became shallow, he took me by the hand and led me into the bedroom.

My nerves were shaky; I had never been with a real man.

"Carrie, I am not going to hurt you, and neither will anybody else. You are safe now."

"I know; I know," I repeated, at a loss for words.

We sat on the edge of our bed totally absorbed in ourselves, gazing at each other, our chests rising and falling in excitement. The tension had us both hypnotized in the moment. Our eyes were locked and didn't blink.

"I don't know if I can do this."

"You can," he encouraged me.

I put total trust in him. He began to undress me, and for the first time since being married, I didn't think about Mr. Camm, and that awful night.

"You all right?" he asked as he slipped my dress over my head.

"I'm ready, Simon," I whispered.

He unhooked my brassiere, and it tumbled to the floor, and then Simon undressed himself in front of me. As I watched, I could barely contain myself, as the temperature rose all over my body. My chest heaved at the sight of him crawling naked up on me, our clothes blanketing the hardwood floor. I trembled, as his breath and tongue traveled the distance of my body, sending chills all over me. When I was ready, twitching and turning, he penetrated his boldness into my juices. We locked our bodies together as one, and for the first time ever, my breath was taken away. It was a beautiful thing.

CHAPTER 3

Nadine from across the street knocked on our door early Saturday morning, less than five minutes after the rooster cocked in the coop out back, and the screech and rumble of wheels from the street trolley interrupted my sleep. The dew was fresh on the ground. I could hear knuckles tapping tirelessly on the wooden door, first soft and then hard. I sucked my teeth and grabbed my housecoat, put it on, and went to the door. There Nadine stood at attention dressed up in a gray skirt and a white blouse, smiling, showing all of her teeth. Her face was draped in big, bouncy curls swinging down over one eye, her full lips gleaming from ruby-red lipstick.

"Excuse me. I know it is early, but I am fresh out of hen eggs, and the corner store is not open yet." She was finely dressed for someone who was about to prepare breakfast. It was like she was headed to church or something. I cracked open the door reluctantly, but she pushed one foot inside, and stood sideways in the door frame, shaking her leg nervously. The orange sun had been waiting to brighten ever since I had laid Robert back down after changing his diaper and giving him his bottle. It was early, too soon for visitors.

"Come in," I said, since she had already inserted her body halfway inside my home.

Nadine boldly stepped inside my kitchen. With a curious eye, she panned the room, scanning her eyes from the ceiling to the floor as if she was looking for something. Nothing was new to her; she'd come over once before when Simon was home to deliver a piece of pound cake she'd made, that was so dry, the bird on the window ledge, tired his beak trying to break it. *Momma said not to eat everybody's cooking.*

"How many eggs do you need?" I asked her.

Twirling impatient fingers through her thick curls, she asked, "Is Simon up yet? I saw him last night when he came home." I suppressed my tongue and thoughts.

"How many eggs do you need?" I asked again.

"Is Simon here?"

"He's sleeping; how many eggs do you

need?" I answered, and opened the icebox. Behind the half-filled jug of milk were the hen eggs I'd gathered the day before from the chicken coop out back. I pulled out four brown eggs. I put them in a brown paper sack and handed them to her. She didn't seem anxious for the eggs, her eyeballs shifting from side to side.

She paused and said, "I thought I'd say hello to Simon since I'm over here," never answering my question.

I put the bag in her hand, but she did not move. I could sense she had something on her mind, but it was too early for me to open up a conversation. I yawned. It was still dusk.

I sort of coaxed her with my hand to the door and said, "We are sleeping in today. I'll tell Simon you said hello."

She gave me a disappointed grin and rolled her eyes. Then she walked out the door. Before she left, she turned toward me. "Thank you! Now don't forget to tell 'em."

As soon as her back cleared the door, I slammed the door shut.

The nerve of her, I thought . . . coming over here all dressed up, and nowhere to go, asking about my husband. It was barely 7 a.m. To have Simon on her heart this early in the morning caused me to be concerned.

She seemed to handle herself like the women Momma warned me about not becoming. "The Floozies," she'd called them. I never wanted to spend too much time around them anyway. When Ms. Pearl arrived in Jefferson, she had taught all the ladies a lesson. I watched as Nadine sashayed out of the yard, and crossed the street. When I was sure Nadine had made it to her front door, I had gone back to my bedroom, and was cuddled up close to my husband, who was sleeping so soundly, he wasn't aware I'd been out of the bed or that Nadine had come by.

When Simon finally rolled over in bed and yawned, I was already up, dressed in my blue, a-line dress, my hair curled under in a page boy bob style and staring blankly out of the bedroom window. I had sat in the huge window seal at dawn and watched the sunrise come over the hill and into the sky. It was panoramic. I could view Nadine's house, the church steeple on the next street and see a glimpse of the steam rising from the factory that made cigarettes and cigars. Now, I knew where all the stacks of tobacco from our farm in Jefferson County ended up. Robert was also awake, staring at me with his clear wide eyes from the pallet I had made for him on the floor. I went into the kitchen, poured myself a hot cup of coffee, with a little cream and a cube of sugar, cooked Simon some strips of bacon and an egg. I felt a bit too mature, now that I had adopted the same routine my momma had followed every morning. I fixed him a plate and sat down. Then I remembered to raise the curtain and tie it back to invite the morning sunshine in to brighten the dullness of the alabaster kitchen walls, which were bare. Everything was neatly kept in drawers and I hadn't come up with anything to decorate the kitchen except the dish towels, which I hand-embroidered our initials on. A skill I'd learned from Momma who embroidered Mrs. Ferguson's napkins and tablecloths.

Outside on the window ledge was a cardinal tweeting and I threw it a kiss, since folks back home said that throwing a kiss at a cardinal would bring good luck. Across the street Nadine and her two children sat on the front porch. Her husband was away on one of his long train trips. He was a porter on the North/South railways.

Simon sat down at the table. "I slept better last night than I have in weeks." I knew this was the truth because the colored baseball players slept anywhere they could. Many times Simon said he slept on the bare wooden floor, or even in the barn with the animals. Just the thought made me nervous.

"You are home; that's why," I said, wiping the minor spill of coffee from the kitchen table.

"Life on the road is hard, Carrie. Just last week I was sleeping on this family's floor and the pallet they made for us was so thin, I felt I was sleeping on the ground. It was rough," he said, touching my shoulders.

"Mama says sleeping on the floor is good for you."

"Maybe, but nothing can take the place of sleeping in a warm bed with my beautiful wife." A wide smile swept across my face, and for a moment, I felt like posing just for him.

After blushing, I laid Robert down on the quilt on the floor. It was away from the stove, but right where I could see him as I finished breakfast and folded clothes.

Simon started to eat, and noticed Nadine out of the window. "Why is she always sitting on the porch? There has got to be some cleaning, cooking or something to do inside," he said, sipping on his coffee.

"Maybe they are not getting done. Maybe she is too busy in other people's business, and sitting on the porch is her way of being nosey," I commented, still a little uptight about her visit early this morning.

"Right . . . she is always staring at us and waving," Simon said, shaking his head.

"Only when you are home, Simon."

"What are you trying to say?"

"Nothing, but something is wrong with her."

"Her husband is gone a lot like I am. She is probably just lonely."

"Maybe so . . ."

"Don't say it like that," he said. "I hate being away from you and Robert."

After breakfast, Simon went outside to gather the eggs from the hens. I watched through the kitchen window as Nadine sat on her front porch twirling her curls with her fingers, and ravenously staring at my husband. She yelled across the road in a long Southern drawl, "Hi, Mr. Simon."

Simon turned and peered at her from across the yard. He waved, but kept moving like she didn't matter. I could see she wanted more, since she stood there grinning and then pacing back and forth on her porch like an anxious school girl. When Simon returned with the eggs, she yelled again, "Thank you for the eggs this mo'ning!"

Simon answered, "Welcome," and walked back into the house.

"What eggs are Nadine talking about? She said we gave her eggs."

"She borrowed some early this morning while you were sleeping."

"Oh," he said, and added, "I told you she wants to be your friend."

"All I have time for is Robert."

Simon was naïve when it came to certain things, or had I just grown up fast. I was nearly eighteen, but I felt much older. I assumed that was why Momma used to say "stay out of grown folks' business. Be careful what you want for because growing up can be painful." From the moment Mr. Camm showed up unannounced at our house, dressed like a city slicker, and told my momma he loved her, and then proved to everyone in the town that he was telling a lie, I learned a lot. And the day the no-good bastard intruded on me, I was forced to grow up. I'd been forced to put away my black doll baby and take care of one of my own. I had Robert now. I didn't understand anything about being a mother. All I learned from playing with the doll was combing hair and pinning a diaper. I felt I had more inside of me than just changing diapers, and cooking food every day.

"Nothing turns out the way you expect it to be," Simon said. "It is not Robert's fault;

he is only a baby. I love him no matter how painfully he came into this world. He is still my boy," he added, tapping his chest, "and I am going to make him a man."

For the most part, Simon was the wiser one, yet I was still baffled. He seemed to overlook things, like answering the letter his sister wrote him over a month ago. And when I mentioned to him how much I miss him, he always felt his desire to be a colored baseball player was so important. His point of view on what was occurring now is more optimistic than real to me. All of my decisions relate directly to what happened to me the last two years. I was young, and tough times were the things I wanted to forget, so I struggled with maturity. My task now was to figure out my future. Would I be a teacher, or settle for taking care of my baby and my man. To add to it all, I believed my life would also include Nadine for some reason. She seemed to have her eyes focused in the wrong direction, and that gave me an uneasy feeling.

Simon was always different and the recollection of me sneaking behind my momma's back to the school yard to see him still remained, in my memory, the best days of my life. He seemed better and more mature than any boy in Jefferson County. I'd watch

Simon when he visited with my brothers, sitting around the kitchen table playing games by candlelight and oil lanterns and secretly wished he could be my boyfriend. And that day when he told me he wanted the same, I felt I was the happiest girl in Jefferson County. Now he was my husband, my knight in shining armor, the one who rescued me from Jefferson County. Now, he was just like the character in the book our teacher Mrs. Miller made us read.

My thoughts had taken me back to a place where I believed only the sun could shine, and a smile had draped my face. It wasn't until Simon asked me, "Are you lonely, Carrie?" that I was snapped back into the present.

"I miss you all the time, especially when you are gone for weeks at a time, so when you are away, I am lonely," I answered, remembering the nights when we first moved to Richmond, and the sounds of the city made me nervous. The cries of the night, the sizzling of steam coming from the street trolleys had replaced the chirping sounds of crickets, and the street light lanterns had brightened the blackness of the night. The empty space on his side of the bed was cold. I was scared. I wanted him near me, snuggled up close to my breasts. I loved the security of having him in the same room.

He smiled. "Nadine's husband is gone too; she would be good company. Maybe she could keep you occupied until I can get back home."

"Nadine's got two children to take care of, and I've got little Robert."

"You need somebody to talk to when I'm away from home."

"I'm doing fine by myself." I didn't need Nadine any more than he did. She was just the lady across the street.

"I hate leaving too, but baseball is my life. I can't wait to play beside Pete Hill or one of them cats. They are some bad colored boys, Carrie. They are three times better than some of them white boys." Simon's almond-shaped eyes lit up when he talked about playing ball, and for a moment, I felt embarrassed because I wanted him home with me.

"Simon, I don't think Nadine and me are alike at all. She's different . . ."

"I just don't want you to feel alone. You need somebody to talk to; that way you want be worrying about me."

"I like Mrs. Hall. She is so good to Robert, and she loves it when we sit on the porch with her."

41

"She's old enough to be yo grandma, and she is white."

"But she is nice, and that is all that matters." In the back of my mind I thought, *and she don't have a longing for my husband.*

"Okay, I thought you and Nadine could talk about husbands and children together. You know, cookin' and things about the house. The kind of things women talk about."

"I am seventeen, and she's at least twenty-five. She's not my type, Simon."

He shook his head, knowing there was no win for this conversation. He changed the subject.

"Let's do something instead of talking about Nadine. Why don't we go downtown today?"

I grinned. I hadn't been downtown but twice since I'd been in Richmond, though it was only several blocks to the east and another few blocks north past the lady dress shop that sold the cloche hats, and pleated chemise dresses I had been hoping to buy one day. The blocks were so much different than the yards of land in the country. Everybody lived feet and not miles away from each other. I loved walking the blocks. The sweet aroma of the food cooking, and the sounds of chatter did something to me.

It did the same thing to Simon too, because I had noticed the grin on his face whenever we spoke to someone sitting on the front porch or steps. The sight of children playing in the streets had both Simon and Robert enthralled, until I coaxed them to come along.

Everyone thought Robert's smile was electrifying. It was a strange thing to say, since I'd never heard anyone from the country mention electricity and smiles. And Robert smiled at everyone we walked past. It was a mild day, and even though the summer was dying and autumn was being birthed, it was around seventy-two degrees. We were walking along, and Robert holding tight to Simon's shoulder when we came across a sign that read, "PEARL BROWN TONIGHT." It was in a bold print and all capital letters.

"Is that the Pearl we know?" I asked.

"She is a nightclub singer," Simon reminded me in a sarcastic manner.

"The last letter I received from Ginny said she was still back home with Willie."

"She's a singer. Jefferson is no place for a person like her. Everybody is trying to get away as soon as they can."

"I just thought she was mourning Camm. He seemed to know how to get the best of everybody." Simon saw the frown lines on my face and the sadness in my hazel eyes. He reached over and put the arm that was free around my neck. Robert and I both depended on his strength.

"Let's not think about him," Simon said, and pulled me in closer.

"You can never be free of the folks you leave behind, can you?"

"Everybody is moving along. Ain't nobody staying the same. You, me, Robert and Ms. Pearl is doing something new. We are free."

The sign was tilted in the window, and the meticulous side of me got the urge to go inside and straighten it out — make it better, but it was only a thought. It was a quaint little club famous for bringing in fresh and new jazz talent to the Heights. We'd heard a few famous folks had been there, but Simon and I had not been anywhere since coming to Richmond, other than to the ice cream bar, for a cup of fresh churned, homemade vanilla cream.

"You want to come back tonight and hear her sing?"

I wasn't sure if I wanted to see her or not. She was the woman seeing my momma's husband, even though he was a sinner when they met. Ms. Pearl hadn't done anything to me, and the one time when we met at the church picnic, she had smiled at me and said I had the prettiest eyes. Momma didn't take too kindly to women like her. She felt a woman should work in the kitchen or for her children. I never heard her mention the bedroom, and I'm certain she didn't believe in anybody singing in anyplace outside of church.

"Yes, I want to go." I replied, "I'll see if Mrs. Hall wouldn't mind watching Robert for me. She is always begging me to leave him with her."

"For us . . .," Simon corrected me.

We walked right past a crowded street trolley hissing along, made the right turn at the corner, a block from the nightclub, and waited in line for an elderly colored lady with high cheekbones to fill our cups with ice cream. If was good, and almost tasted as good as Momma's, but she didn't have strawberries. Robert's eyes widened at the sight of the cup. We sat at the counter along with other free-minded colored people. Back home, colored-people were only farmers, and sitting at an ice cream counter was unheard of. Richmond was surely different from the country; colored people strutted instead of walking bent over, hiding their faces from the white man. It was a sight to see.

CHAPTER 4

Simon and I arrived around 7:30, just as a black Studebaker pulled up and let out banker, Mrs. Maggie Walker. People recognized the car and rushed in closer to see her. Simon and I watched nearby at the spectators smiling and waving at her. Simon stood straight up with his mouth wide open, gawking at the shiny, black new Studebaker. "You like that car, Carrie?"

"Yes," I answered, anxiously waiting to catch a glimpse of the famous Maggie Walker. When she got out of the car, she was taller than me, and her light-yellow skin smoother and softer in appearance than what I'd expected. She had me mesmerized. I'm not sure what I thought she'd look like, but she was not the person I'd envisioned. She had a gregarious smile and shook hands with anybody who dared to walk up to her. I stood glued to the stone pavement. I wanted to do the same, but my feet wouldn't move — felt like I was carrying around bricks on my feet.

The air was thin and fresh, and every star in the sky was out and in place. The colored folks were exquisitely dressed, the ladies with dropped-waist chiffon dresses embellished with sequins and pleats. The men wore church suits and hats. It was a parade of beautiful people walking in with their backs as straight as a pole, demanding the attention of those of us eager to get a glimpse of the new fashions I could only dream about.

I had never been in a place like this. I didn't think I was old enough to be there, but who could turn us away, a married woman and her husband. The one time I'd been in a place similar was when I was in Jefferson County and my momma let me go with her to hunt down her drunken husband. We went to the joint and she told me, "Now sit out here. I've got a few questions to ask." Once she was inside, I got out of the wagon and peeked in the side window. It was full of a bunch of church folks drinking whiskey and some of them were drunk and leaning sideways in their chairs. But, when Momma returned, she said to me, "Now this is no place for a lady. Only floozies hang around this place." She helped her drunken, "corn liquor seeping out from his pores" husband into the wagon, and we went home.

This place was different, though. The patrons were businesslike. The dungarees had been replaced with trousers, ironed and creased. The women Momma called floozies were business owners, and leaders in Jackson Heights. It was a warm place. And, I fit in just like the rest of the ladies. I had on my same tan dress, but it had been altered and updated once I saw how the ladies dressed in Richmond. I made it into a dropped waist by cutting the bottom of the dress below my hips and sewing on black fabric I had pinned into pleats. It was as pretty as the rest of the dresses, and it was a tailored fit. I'm so glad Momma had taught me how to sew. My hair was curled under, and I had on a little rouge and pink lipstick. "You look like a China doll, baby," Simon whispered to me at the club. Mrs. Hall had already told me I looked like a grown woman instead of the teenager I was. Simon was as dapper as the men coming into the club. He had on a dark-brown suit with a bowtie. This was the first time ever I'd seen him dressed this well. He almost looked like Mr. Camm, but I reminded myself how most men in the city dressed distinguished.

The money Simon had made on the road could possibly have been spent in one place, yet he was frugal. He ordered us both a Pepsi-Cola, and we snacked on the complimentary peanuts already in a dish on the walnut-stained tables. Through the dim light, we gazed at each other passionately. There was something mystical about the lights being low. I felt vulnerable, and maybe even sexy. Simon eyed me intensely, like he could bite me, and I blushed and smiled like a Cheshire cat. The place was beautiful. Each of the tables had a lamp, the low light casting a romantic glow and my Simon gazing at me like he had something he wanted to say.

"You all right?" Simon asked.

"Yes. This is so exciting! I ain't ever been in a place like this," I said, looking around and admiring the faces and fashions of the beautiful people.

He put his arm around me. He appeared comfortable, relaxed in this atmosphere. He was more like the patrons than different.

"Have you ever been here?" I tried to resist asking him, knowing I might get jealous of his answer.

"I've been here before."

It was not the answer I expected to hear, although I could tell he was in familiar territory. So, I got a little concerned.

"Were you alone?"

"No, I came with a few cats from the team. When we come in town, we occasionally get dressed, and have a drink."

I didn't know my husband was a drinker of anything outside of Pepsi and water.

"This is not something I do all the time," he added, "and it is not the kind of place you should come to by yourself," he said, smiling and pointing. It was as if he were giving orders to me. It was more like a fatherly lecture than one of a husband.

"I'm nervous; do you think I will fit in?"

"Sure. These people are no better than you," he assured me.

"It ain't that many country girls in here, I can tell. Most of them hold their drinks differently, and the women sit with their legs crossed instead of their feet crossed at the ankles."

He chuckled. "People are people. Country folks are like city folks; they just have different chores to do."

"The women remind me of my teacher, Mrs. Miller. She always had on a variety of dresses. She wasn't plain like me."

"Tonight, you look like the rest of the women in here, but better," he said.

A girlish smile swept across my face, and I

could feel my cheeks reddening. I no longer needed the rouge on my cheeks.

The club filled up quickly. All the seats at the tables were taken and most of the wooden stools around the bar. Ms. Pearl could definitely fill a room. Everyone chatted and listened to the soft sounds, eager to get a glimpse of the singer. Mrs. Maggie Walker sat at the table right in front at center stage. All of the people at her table seemed to carry a certain demeanor. They appeared confident and relaxed. All of them were dressed so dapper, I had to stare. The black suits and bowties made the men stand out, and the ladies had fitted chiffon dresses of all colors. Simon and I were somewhere in the middle, but close enough to see everything that was taking place. I was jittery since this was my first time.

At ten minutes past nine o'clock, in walked Ms. Pearl. She took long, deliberately slow strides straight up to the microphone in the middle of the stage. It was as if she were a swan, the way she glided and strolled delicately through the tables and up the side stairs to the middle of the stage. The crowd roared at the sight of her, and I started to sweat like a nervous little kid. I knew she was famous, but not this famous. Everybody stood up and the applause seemed to grow louder and stronger. Simon smiled and clapped his hands so vigorously his palms turned a bright pink.

Ms. Pearl stood in the middle of the stage smiling and posing. The red chiffon dress she had on with sequins on the pleats fit her like a Sunday glove. Every curve on her body was highlighted, and her dress sparkled. Her makeup was flawless. The nutmeg powder and the rouge on her cheeks gave her a burst of color. She seemed too beautiful to have ever lived in Jefferson County.

"Good evening, beautiful people!" she said in her sultry Southern accent.

The crowd answered, "Good evening to you too, Mz. Pearl!"

She pulled the microphone close to her rose-red lips and bellowed out some of the deepest tones I'd ever heard. Her voice was rich and heart-wrenching. When she started to sing, it sounded like every word flowed right from her heart and everyone felt it. She stood tall and statuesque demanding the ears of the patrons. Those who were chatting before she appeared on stage were engrossed soulfully into her rhythm. They clapped, and some stood up while others swayed from left to right. Simon and I both bobbed our heads. A few people danced in the aisles. Simon took my hand. "Want to dance?" I couldn't dance, but I'd always wanted to. So, I grabbed his waiting hand and we went to the center of the hardwood dance floor, in the middle of the tables. I laid my head on his broad chest, and we both closed our eyes and inhaled the music to the fullest, along with the cigar smoke.

We moved from side to side to the music.

"How do you feel?" Simon asked me.

"Good, just a little nervous."

"What's wrong?"

"I've never danced in front of anybody," I whispered to him.

"I like how you dance."

We swayed cheek to cheek. It was warm. Beads of sweat popped out on my forehead. I was dancing for the first time alongside bankers and educators, and strangely, I was shy.

As we turned to walk back through the crowd to our seats, I noticed Pearl gazing down at us, and when I glanced up at her, she grinned. I didn't know how to act. It was a warm and cold feeling. The warmth came from seeing someone you know perform in front of an ignited crowd, with cheeks blushing with jubilation. I felt proud. The cold came from the reputation folk back home prefaced her with before speaking of her. Folk in Jefferson County were

53

like that.

The dimly lit room was the perfect setting for the sounds she delivered. The shadows of bobbing heads reflected along the wall. After Ms. Pearl had bellowed out the final tune with a thunder of applause, she sashayed down the stairs past the sophisticated crowd and came right toward us. She got to the table so fast that when I looked up, there she stood as straight as an arrow smiling down seductively at Simon and me.

Simon hopped up. "Hi, Ms. Pearl. Won't you have a seat?"

"Hi," I said, my eyes fixated on her oval face and flawless beauty.

"What are y'all folk doing up here, in Richmond?" she asked.

"We live here now," Simon answered.

The folks at the table beside us peered from across the way at her as if she had more importance than Mrs. Maggie Walker. We seemed to gain some of that importance by association. Ms. Pearl knew they were watching too, because she waved cunningly at the staring man, and grinned. His wife smiled too.

"So y'all done moved away from Jefferson . . . that place is for old people and folk with no desires," she jokingly said.

"We like it here," Simon told her.

"I like it too. But it is just a stop on my way to New York City," she stated with authority, still standing, towering over our table. As we looked up, we could see her large breasts oozing out of her dress. She was provocative, her top almost as skimpy as the young vaudeville singer everyone was talking about, Josephine Baker, who was gaining fame from dancing in shows all across the Midwest.

"We are going to be here awhile," Simon commented.

"Richmond is nice, and I love it in Jackson Heights, but Washington is the place with all the money."

"Yes, ma'am," I said, trying to add to the conversation.

"You don't have to call me ma'am. I ain't that old."

I smiled knowing anybody in their thirties was old to me.

"How's that baby of yours?"

"He is good; just growing so fast."

"Does he favor his daddy?"

A frown rolled over Simon's face, and I sucked my teeth.

Simon didn't wait for me to answer her. He said, "He looks just like us."

"Good, because that son-of a bitch didn't deserve a child."

If he was so bad, then why did you sneak around with him? He was a married man. The thoughts were there, but the words wouldn't come out. I held my lips tight.

"Look, I want y'all to come back to check me out. It is nice to see familiar faces in the room."

"We'll be back," Simon said.

As she turned to walk away, her husband, Willie, walked over to the table.

"Who is this?"

"They are from Jefferson," she answered.

"How's everybody doing?" he asked, and shook Simon's hand first and then mine.

I had heard Ginny say he was a stunningly handsome man, and he was a big chocolate man with a beautiful smile and dark eyes. He appeared strong, but he dressed like a lot of the men from Jefferson. He was in a dark suit with shined brogan boots. It was as close as he came to being a city man. They were an attractive couple. It was unfortunate she had spent most of her time in the arms of Herman Camm, a selfish man who did not care for anyone, but himself.

"Now I want to see y'all back here soon. I am going to be performing here every Saturday night."

"We will be back," Simon replied.

56

I didn't say anything because I had hoped to get away from Ms. Pearl, Herman Camm, and all the memories of Jefferson County. Now, I was wondering if I could ever put the past behind me. Would I always run into people like Ms. Pearl?

"Let's go," Simon said.

When we turned to walk away, I felt at ease. We left the handsome couple standing at our table. Just before we left the building I took one last look, and Ms. Pearl was already doing what she did best, titillating the crowd, leaning over the tables, smiling, and mesmerizing everybody around. Willie was not beside her anymore, but was standing off to the side watching her every move. As always, the men were hypnotized by her beauty and stature, and the women were sucking in their teeth because she'd once again stolen their husband's or boyfriend's attention. She even had that way with Simon. I was glad we were going home. She was a dangerous woman.

CHAPTER 5

Simon was already undressed and lying in between my thighs before I remembered the vinegar sponge Mrs. Hall had given me. It was my security. Getting pregnant was not an option for me, since Simon was traveling around with the Colored League, and I had decided I couldn't raise another child alone. Tonight had happened too fast. With each kiss, he inserted his tongue deeper down my throat. After that, his tongue panned over my body, landing on my heavy breasts. The sensation was so heated. When his lips touched my neck, and then my breasts and belly button, I was lost. I trembled all over with pleasure, and my body locked with intensity. His eyes fixated on my bare body, my full breasts dancing with the rhythm. And I gazed at him, staring at his beautiful body, his manhood erect and thick. He was hungry. I let him have his way with me touching and thrusting inside me, and then

I rolled on top and galloped uncontrollably until he was full on me. As he placed his lips on mine, I swallowed, my memory became foggier, and it took my breath away.

I knew he'd be going away soon, and perhaps it was the reason I didn't get up early the next morning. Instead I sank myself comfortably into Simon's warm arms until Robert let out a desperate cry. After Robert was fed, he played on the pallet I'd made for him on the floor. When Simon started putting his things together in a duffle bag, I knew he was about to leave.

"It is time, isn't it?" I asked him, watching him neatly pack his shirts and pants into the bag he'd gotten downtown.

He glanced over at me. "Why, Carrie, do you say this every time?"

"I just hate it when you leave."

"One day it won't be like this. I'm a country boy chasing a dream."

His comment got to me. I felt the heat on my scalp, so I locked my lips to prevent from lashing out at him. It had been three months since Simon had spent more than a few days with us.

"I'm a country girl in the city trying to raise a baby all by myself."

"Come on now — you are not alone."

"You are not here, Simon. The folks

around here don't know me. They just help out because they feel sorry for Robert and me."

He kept folding his clothes, but with the tightening of his face, I could see he was getting annoyed, so much so that he didn't look my way.

I continued, "I want you to stop with the Colored League. Don't anybody care about a league of colored boys traveling from place to place. White people will not come to see colored boys play."

"I care! And, so should you."

I had struck a nerve. Simon and I never argued about anything, but time after time, I'd pushed back tears and held my tongue when he was walking out of the door. Afterward, I felt hurt and sorry because I had not let him know my feelings. Things were about to change.

"I care. I just don't want to be here in a strange city alone."

"All of us colored boys are gone from home. I miss you too, but you know how much I love the game. I am going to play with Pete Hill one day and some of them other colored greats."

When the Independent Team came to Richmond, the whole Jackson Heights community went over to the park to see them play. Simon performed that day. He hit a ball over everybody's head and straight out of the field. The ball came close to hitting one of the white people standing in the road watching. I recall a man sitting behind me saying, "Now that colored boy can play some ball. He might be as good as Pete one day." Some of the other men agreed. I stuck my chest out and an uncontrollable smile rippled across my face. Now I couldn't help myself. I wanted him home more than I wanted to see his dreams fulfilled.

"Okay," I mumbled.

"Is that all you can say, Carrie?"

"What do you want me to say?"

"I was hoping you'd say you support me and understand."

"I do."

He stood gazing at me in disappointment, his magnetic smile completely absent from his face, and our little Robert staring at us from the pallet on the floor as if he knew something was going wrong.

"I really do understand," I assured him. It was the same yearning I had to become a teacher. I'd wanted to teach from the very first time I stepped foot into the one-room schoolhouse in Jefferson County. I admired how Mrs. Miller stood in front of the classroom demanding we grasp the proper

English language and applauding us when we learned. I so much wanted to be like her. She cared about people. Everyone in her family had been educated. If Papa had lived, I would have had a different life. I was convinced of it.

Simon read my scorched heart, and came over to me. He put his arms around me, but I couldn't do the same. I couldn't give in to his notion. "Carrie, it will get easier with time. Pretty soon you are not going to miss me this way."

After a moment, filled with emotion, I gazed into his eyes and softened. I loosened up, and slid my arm around his waist.

"I'll be all right. I guess I have a lot to learn about being married."

"You already know about it. It is hard for me too."

As he reached down to pick up Robert, I couldn't help wondering if he meant it was hard because he had more responsibility with me and Robert, or that getting the leagues attention was tough. Whatever the case, I was going to be the one left alone to raise Robert. Seemed to me I was growing up too fast.

Simon always held Robert in his arms and played with him before he left. Perhaps he felt embarrassed about leaving him. Robert cooed and held tight to his shirt. At times, Simon appeared to want to say something to Robert; however, he was too young to understand. He'd stare at him — straight in the eyes. Robert would just smile. It was a stressful day for me. Two days home and Simon was back on the road.

When he and Robert went into the bedroom, I knew exactly what he was doing. As usual, he was stuffing a wad of money under my bed pillow. It was always enough to pay the rent, buy food and a little extra, which I put away in a cigar box underneath the bed for a rainy day.

When Simon was done packing and stashing money like he'd done every trip, he put Robert back on the floor and took my hand. We sat down on the soft davenport.

"Everything I do is for us."

"I know," I said, "just don't like to see you leave."

"Carrie, you know I love you. So why is this so hard to deal with?"

"Because I don't want to raise Robert alone."

"I'm with you, girl; just can't be home all the time."

"I know, Simon," was my only response.

Simon got up from the davenport, and again grabbed my hand. He pulled me so close my chest heaved for air. He placed his lips over mine and kissed me so deep, I could feel the moisture.

"I'll be back in a week, Carrie. Be strong. Remember we didn't come to Richmond to fail."

He picked up his duffle bag, and moved toward the door. I walked alongside him, keeping pace with his long strides. The closer we got to the door, the harder it was to hold back the tears welling up in the corners of my eyes. After he kissed me goodbye, I stood in the doorway and watched him walk down the stairs into the street. Tearfully, I sat in my large bedroom-window seat and my eyes followed his car all the way up the street and into the brush of trees and out of sight.

CHAPTER 6

Simon had been away for more than a week when an unexpected visitor knocked on my door. Momma came wearing a new hat and a smile as wide as the James River. Seeing her smile was something abnormal for me. Her serious demeanor had been how people related to her. But after six months, she had changed drastically. And, it was possibly for the good. When she wrote me letting me know she'd be paying me a visit, I didn't think it would be a week later. Ironically, she showed up the same day I received Simon's disturbing letter. It said he would be traveling to Baltimore, to play the Black Sox, and then on to Kansas City before returning home. He said they wanted to go to Chicago, but after the race war of 1919, the league was afraid to go in that direction. People were being lynched for crossing the invisible territorial race lines. Old Rube Foster was still pushing though for the

Major League to recognize the colored teams.

Momma's smile was inviting, yet her comments were still negative. After she put her bag in my room and placed her new black hat neatly on my vanity, she came into the kitchen. She sat down at the kitchen table. With Robert in one arm, and a cup of coffee in the other, she said, "You know Jefferson County ain't changed much since you left."

"Oh yeah . . . ," I commented, and the intensity of her gaze stayed the same.

I could sense she was expecting to gain knowledge of something from me. She'd pause, waiting for a reaction from me, but I had nothing to say. The news about Jefferson was not surprising. I continued sipping on my steaming hot coffee, blowing it occasionally.

Finally, she said, "White folks still don't like coloreds. They're still talking about lynching us and killing us."

I couldn't understand why all of a sudden, the social environment of Jefferson was something of interest. "Momma, I really don't care much about Jefferson. I am in Richmond now. I've got to run my life from where I am. Besides, white people run this country. Colored folk are going to be second class until we get us an education."

Her brows heightened and her eyes grew concerned. "You should care."

"I don't understand what you mean," I said, raising my voice and shaking my head.

"Now listen here!" Her voice grew stronger. "You don't have no reason to sass me," she said, her eyes pouring into me like an arrow. "I am letting you know that white people are the same everywhere, even here in Richmond."

Her comments got to me and I struggled to keep from disrespecting her. "I don't have anything to do with no white people in Jefferson. They been treating people bad all their lives; they ain't going to change in a few months."

"Hush yo mouth, chile!"

"What are you talking about, Momma? Just tell me."

The room was quiet. Even little Robert didn't make a sound. He looked at her, his bright eyes fixated on the grimace that was taking over her face.

"Why are you allowing a white woman to look after your child?" she boldly asked.

I thought about what she'd said for a moment. "Why is everybody so scared of the white man?"

She rested her hand on her fist. "You need

to make sure you understand what they will do to you before you let that lady take care of your child."

I didn't want to talk about Mrs. Hall.

"Momma, I want to know how Ginny is doing. She is somebody that matters. I wrote her a letter, and haven't heard back from her yet," I said, changing the subject.

"Ginny is doing good. I saw her at church last Sunday. She asked about you and Robert as she always does. Lord knows she claims she don't get around much, but she is always at church."

"I miss her," I said.

"I know she misses you. Nobody goes around there to see her much. Minnie's children visit, but they don't have the kind of relationship you had with her."

The transition of our conversation from white folks to Ginny was something we both could speak about, and we needed it as much as an autumn breeze. Besides, Ginny had been on my mind, had been in my dreams and thoughts for over a week. I couldn't forget the coffee and buttered biscuits she'd offered me right before filling my head with the kind of wisdom I never got from Momma, but longed for as any teenager would.

Momma began by giving me a rundown

of all the people in the county. She started with Ginny and how her arthritis had kept her down for two months until she took a dose of turmeric, and then on to Pearl, who had moved and making most of the women in Jefferson happy, since she was never a settled woman — rather one who moved from man to man. It was more information than I'd ever expected from her. When I lived with Momma, she was tight-lipped and so guarded that she made me feel distant. She never revealed much to anyone, including my papa who shared his heart with everybody around. This was not expected. She even said the preacher had been coming over to her house to see about her. She said he'd been helping Carl with some of the outside work. Maybe he was the one responsible for the smile she had on her face when I opened the front door. I remember her having that same smile after Papa died.

"Carrie, do Nadine come over here much to see you?"

Momma remembered Nadine from the letter I'd written her the second week I was in Richmond. I'd described all of my neighbors to her. I wanted her to know how they looked and smiled. My excitement was written on each line of all the letters I'd written to her. So, it was no surprise she recognized my neighbors even though she had not officially met them.

"No, ma'am, she don't."

"She is close to your age."

"We are different, though."

"What on earth does that mean, chile?"

"She is just not my type of friend."

Before Momma could comment, there was a knock on the door. I sighed when I peeped out of the door, and it was Nadine.

"Come in," I said.

"The children say you got a visitor over here. Simon must be in town."

Momma sipped on her coffee and listened to the conversation before she said anything.

"Well, hello, Nadine," she said. "Most peoples come in the house usually know to speak."

"I'm sorry, ma'am. I just came in the door talking," Nadine assured her, smiling.

She then walked over to Momma, and reached to shake her hand. Momma stood up and shook her hand.

Afterward, Nadine said, "I have never seen you before. You related to Carrie?"

"Yes, she's my child."

"Oh, okay. You live in Jefferson?"

"I do," Momma answered.

"Well, my little boy said somebody was over here, so I stopped by to see. I thought

70

Simon was back in town."

Momma didn't wait for me to say anything. She quickly commented, "You married, Nadine?" she asked.

"Yes, ma'am."

"It seems mighty strange for a married woman to be asking about somebody else's husband."

"My husband works on the railroad," she said, shying away from Momma's comment.

Momma glanced over at me. I didn't open my mouth, sort of enjoying the way Momma had addressed Nadine.

"Nadine, when will your husband be home?" Momma asked.

"I don't know no more. He comes whenever he wants to. I never know anything."

"You had best to stay ready in case he come home soon."

"I guess," Nadine commented. "I guess I ought to get on across the road now . . . nice meeting you, ma'am," she said as she walked toward the door.

"You, too!" Momma replied.

After Nadine was out of the door, Momma looked at me. "You got yourself a Pearl Brown right across the road. You keep your eyes open. That chile is bold. She seems to be trouble."

Nadine didn't have me fooled. I could tell

what she was up to the day she borrowed the eggs.

Having Momma with me in Richmond for two weeks was good for me and Robert. Momma rose early. She enjoyed seeing the breaking of dawn, since she felt God was able to speak to her best in total solitude. It was the time to talk to the Lord, she'd say. It was good for me because it was obvious Robert felt the same way. He always woke early, and after a changing of his diaper and a bottle of milk, he'd go back to sleep until the sun was at its fullest. It was the first time since he'd been in the world I was able to get a full night's sleep.

Simon's absence made me nervous. I had never lived alone. I was surrounded by families I barely knew. However, Momma's presence relieved me of the anxiety of being totally responsible for the care of my son. Momma did everything for him. She watched him while I sashayed to the store free as a bird. And, because she was watching him, I took my time. I'd go up and down every aisle in the store. I knew which aisle the pickled beets were on and how the shortening was stuck between the flour and sugar. On the way home, I held my head back and let the autumn breeze kiss my face. It was like I was new. Momma fed

Robert, played with him and lay down beside him until he fell off to sleep. She smiled at everything Robert did. She even grinned when she took off his diaper, and he squirted pee in her face and on her glasses. She gave him all the attention she had not given my brothers and me. We never understood why she was so cold, and detached from us, but now she was different. She treated Robert as if he mattered. And when I caught her kissing him on the cheek, I was at a loss for words.

"We are getting used to you being here with us," I told her after unloading the sack I brought home with sugar, flour and butter for the cake she'd been promising to bake before she went home.

"I am going home in two days. I've been here long enough. My house is left unattended to. Carl has been too busy with his own land. He got to finish that other room they are building for the children."

"What children, Momma? Is Mary expecting?"

"No, not yet, but they are young. I told 'em they had plenty of time, but Mary wanted to get a room ready, just in case."

"Carl is a good husband. He will do anything to please Mary."

"Simon's good too! He took you and Robert in without any questions. A man like that is hard to find. Lord knows he reminds me of my Robert. That man worked hisself to death. Now, he was a good man. Lawd, if I only knew."

Momma was profound with her statement. My papa was a great man, yet she only smiled for a snake walking on legs. That was strange to me, since he treated her like shit.

CHAPTER 7

I left Robert sleeping beside Momma soon after the rooster crowed and I got a peek at daybreak. I couldn't let her catch the train back to Jefferson before I handled some business of my own. I got dressed and took some coins for the trolley out of the household cash that Simon always left behind. It was a brisk morning; the trees in the yard were swaying with the breeze. The sun was a deep bronze, transforming the landscape and growing brighter with each step I took. The cobblestone walkway was hard on the dress shoes I was wearing. It was quiet outside, totally peaceful. As I absorbed the beauty of downtown Broad Street, I couldn't help daydreaming about teaching in the schoolhouse I passed by on the way downtown. Just the thought cast a smile on my face.

I couldn't help noticing how the trees had started to turn colors. The buildings were old and colonial with large columns. When I walked right past the John Marshall hotel which had been the lodging place for the president and other dignitaries, I slowed my pace in hopes of seeing someone of importance, but the only person around was a doorman in a top hat, and he didn't even smile. There was something special about Richmond and I loved the buildings and how they towered over the city with authority. The white folks stared at me. One gazed so long I thought she might pop an eye vessel, but not one of them stepped off the sidewalk or acted like I was an animal, like I'd seen happen in front of the Seed and Feed store in Jefferson. The white folk in Jefferson felt we black people had a disease; at least they acted like it, despite the fact that some colored women were wet nurses for white children. The Richmond Whites appeared used to the colored folks and we seemed used to them. Some of the merchants in Jackson Heights were even friends with many of them. Not all colored folks were servants and laborers. Besides, my papa told me I was as smart and important as the whites were.

As I continued to the trolley station, I couldn't help wondering about Ms. Pearl and what would happen if she and Momma were to see each other on the street. Would they speak? Or would they scrabble? I know Momma didn't like Pearl, and thus it was hard for me to like her. But, when we heard her sing at the club, she was nice to me and appeared better than all the stories people told. I took the trolley down near Virginia Union Normal School, and got off and walked the three blocks to the campus. There were only a few students on the yard.

A man came up and introduced himself to me. "Hi, I am Adam Murphy." Adam was about my age, studying to become a minister at Virginia Union. He was a dark fellow with light-brown eyes, a fine bridged nose and full lips. He was what I'd call a distinguished-looking, beautiful man. He was polite as well.

"I'm Carrie," I said. "I'm here trying to find out about taking classes."

"So, you want to be a minister?"

"No, I'm interested in teaching," I answered, admiring his enunciation of each syllable, taking me back to Mrs. Miller and her deliberate repetitions in sounding out vowels.

"I can take you to the office, but most people who want to teach go to the Virginia Normal School in Petersburg."

As we walked toward the building where

the administration office was, I felt comfortable asking him about school. And he didn't mind giving me advice, pointing out the buildings and speaking with confidence about being a student.

"How far is Petersburg from here?" I asked.

"It is not far. The train can get you there in thirty minutes. Most of the people I know go there on Sunday and return home on Thursday evening. Many of the students stay in rooming houses."

"I don't have money for a room. I don't know why I thought I could go to school." The money Simon left each month was only enough to maintain our apartment with a little left over. And I'd been saving it for school.

The closer we got to the front door of the brick building, the faster my heart was beating, tiny beads of sweat popping up on my nose. I was jittery. The building was the home of the administrators and classrooms. I'd heard about college from my brother, John, and everything he said was exciting, but being married and with a child, I knew for me it would not be the same. This was the first time I'd made a decision on my own in my life. I decided I wanted to go to school and for some reason felt it would happen. The fellow added, "Most of us have to work. The school will help you with a job if you can't find one on your own. I work right here on the yard. I help keep the grounds. It's not a big position, but it helps pay for school and gives me a little extra."

"That's encouraging." I said, thinking I could make do with any amount of money. Country girls knew how to make their own clothes and all I wanted was a safe place for Robert and me to stay during the week and enough money for food. The thought of me making a decision without Simon was scary. Even though I hated it when Simon packed his bags to go back on the road, I sincerely admired him. He knew what he wanted to do and nothing, not even his family, could prevent him from pursuing his goals. I was a bit selfish.

The schoolhouse was a mansion compared to the one I'd received my learning in. It was a brick building off the road, isolated just for education. Adam escorted me right up to the office. It was as if he'd known me and agreed I needed to be in school. As I waited to speak to the lady in the glasses sitting behind the desk, he excused himself. "I'll be outside waiting for you."

I was the only girl in the line. I finally got my turn to sit down and speak to the lady, who appeared to be stressed by the questions asked by the fellow ahead of me. "What can I do for you, young lady?" she asked, with a little frown on her face.

"I want to go to school and become a teacher. Can you help me?"

"This is not a school for teachers. Most of the students here come to learn about religion and the sciences."

"Ma'am, I want to teach school."

"You need to go down to Petersburg. I will give you a referral. They will get you enrolled and you will be on your way."

"Are there students in school with babies?"

"You got a baby?"

"Yes, ma'am. My son is eight months old."

"Who is going to help you watch him?"

"I was going to take him with me."

"Going to school is not easy. You will have to give your full attention to your studies. Can your momma help you with the child?"

"We don't have family here, only my husband, and he is away most of the time."

"You are going to need some help, dear. Schooling is not easy. You are going to at least need someone during the week. The classes at the Normal School meet three, sometimes four, days a week. I will give you a name over there. She will help you get enrolled. But, listen, dear, you are going to have to find someone to sit with your baby. Like I said, schooling is hard."

"Yes, ma'am," I said, and got up to leave. She handed me a piece of paper with a name and address on it. Before I could leave, she said, "Now cheer up your face. You can do it. Women have it hard, seeing to the children and all, but anything you want badly enough, you can do."

"Thank you," I said, and turned to walk away.

She reached out to me and stroked my forearm. "Now come back to see me after you get that teacher's diploma and I will help you find a job."

When I left her, I had tears of joy and concern dripping out the corners of my eyes.

I wiped them before I made it to the door. I didn't want Adam to see the me that way.

"You all right?" he asked.

"I'm fine," I lied.

He walked me across the grounds and into the street. It was a comfort having this stranger with me and disappointing that I had not been honest with him. Adam told me where he lived, which was across the road from Union College. I told him I'd stop by when I could. He asked where I lived, but I ignored him both times.

When I made it back to my house, Mrs. Hall was on the porch even though the summer season had started to change. The extremely warm days became cool with breezy nights. The coolness was perfect for a good night's sleep. When she saw me dressed up in my Sunday dress and shoes, she couldn't resist commenting.

"Where have you been? You look very nice."

"Thank you!" I answered.

"Well, where have you been all dressed up?" Aside from being nice, Mrs. Hall was also inquisitive. Momma said she was a nosey white lady. Momma had witnessed Mrs. Ferguson, the lady she worked for, listening to her husband and a few other men at the barn door one evening. She told Momma it was best to know what was going on for yourself rather than to hear the story from a man, who often fudged the truth.

"I have been to town. I went to see about going to school."

"What kind of school you talking about? A lot of people trying to get to the Madam CJ Walker school of beauty, and learn how to do hair."

"I want to teach school."

"Well, you are certainly smart enough," she said. "I taught a class or two in my day too.

I didn't expect her to react positively about school since most colored folk worked as servants in white folks' homes and education was not something they supported.

"What are you going to do with little Robert if you decide to go school?"

It was as if she had been reading my mind. Robert is all I'd had thoughts about the entire trolley ride and walk home. Would he know I was gone? I hoped he would not feel like I didn't love him. How could I go to school with a son? How could I take him with me? How would Simon handle it all? Would I be able to study and raise a child? All of these had been questions I needed to provide answers to.

"I don't know, Mrs. Hall. I want him to go with me. He is my child. I've got to figure things out."

"We are here for you. I know it is hard to be out in the world alone. Look at me. I'm a white woman with a big colored husband and living with him in a colored community. Yes, indeed, I know what it feels like to be alone."

Momma was up in the window watching me. With her hands she was coaxing me to come on in.

"I have to get on upstairs. My momma has had Robert all morning."

"If you need somebody to help with Robert while you are in school, we are here. Colored folk have been deprived for too long. You need to get your education and help other coloreds get ahead. Right, Mr. Hall . . ."

"Yes, ma'am," I answered, thinking about what Mrs. Hall had just said and her offer to take care of Robert.

Momma was frustrated when I returned.

"You've been out all morning. Where have you been, chile?"

"I went to check on a school. I was going to be a teacher."

"You ain't got no time for teaching. You have a baby to take care of and a husband now. You need to get all of that out of your head."

"Momma, I thought you wanted me to get an education," I said as I sat down at the kitchen table.

"I did before you went and got yourself pregnant."

"You still don't get it, do you?" I asked as the tears rolled down my cheeks.

"I know it really wasn't your fault, but I don't understand why you can't be happy being a wife and mother."

Everything she was saying was disturbing to me. I had expected more. As a child, she'd encouraged my brothers and me to learn as much as possible. Now she was telling me to be a mother and accept my responsibilities, forget about school.

I wiped my tears with the back of my hand, sucked my teeth and tried to find the correct words.

"I want Robert to be proud of me. I want to teach colored folk how to read and get a skill. I want to be there for him in every way. I want him to see me as a strong woman who does not live in the shadow of a man."

"What? We woman should take care our children and our homes first. You don't want your responsibility. You took off out of here this morning without asking me to watch your son. You are going down the wrong road, I tell you. Simon is off working for you, and you are out in this big city looking for a way to stay away from home and go to school."

Every word flowing from her mouth was negative. She had a smile on her face, but was still as rigid as ever. I hated disrespecting her like I had the many times in Jefferson County, sneaking up to the school yard with

85

Simon, allowing him to rub his hands up and down my stockings.

"I am a responsible momma!" I raised my voice.

"Well, why did you go out this morning chasing a dream you know don't make a bit of sense."

"I *am* going to school, Momma, and I *will* be a teacher!" I shouted back at her knowing at anytime she could slap me sick.

"You need to try to hold on to your husband. He is a good man taking on you and Robert. Now Nadine is waiting to get next to him and you running off to chase your dreams is a bunch of mess. Good women don't do things like this."

"Momma, please! How long are you going to put me down?"

"I'm not putting you down. I don't want you to be without a husband. Somebody to take care of you . . ."

"Robert and I will be just fine. Mrs. Hall said she'd help me with him."

"You can't trust no white woman, I told you. She don't want to see about a colored child. Are you losing your mind?"

"No."

"Well. If you think a white woman gonna take care of a colored child, you are fooling yourself."

"I believe her. She and Mr. Hall help me all the time."

"You need to stay from down there. I seen ya standing there talking like they were in the family. You don't know them."

"No, ma'am, I don't. I know you, though, and everything you have said has been mean. You don't have any faith in me. You have always turned your back on the truth. When Papa was living, you never showed him any love, but you giggled and took care of another man. I don't understand you. Right now, Mrs. Hall is being more of a mother to me than you have ever been."

"You don't know what you are talking about. I should have left you where I found you," she said.

Again tears filled up my eyes. I reached over and grabbed Robert out of her arms. She sat there with a blank stare on her face, like I had done something so irritating she couldn't move.

I did feel bad. I had never talked to my momma like that before.

"Momma, please pack your bags and get the hell out of my house!" I shouted.

It didn't feel right saying those things to my momma. I had held my feelings in for too long. And, from her words, she'd done the same. Momma jumped up and went into the bedroom. After a few minutes, she came out of the bedroom, with her bags packed, and headed to the depot to take the evening train back to Jefferson County.

She walked out the door and down the street without saying goodbye, her head stuck high in the sky. She didn't even wave goodbye.

CHAPTER 8

I ran in to Pearl Brown all dressed up in a canary-yellow dress leaning on the arm of a tall, slender, distinguished-looking white man. They were coming out of the Jefferson Hotel one morning at the corner of Broad and Adams Street. It was strange seeing a colored woman clinging so tightly to a white man, and I was not the only one staring in my shoes. I glanced around and noticed two colored men whispering like women. Several white men standing in a huddle gave them a stern look, but neither Pearl nor the man seemed bothered. I was on my way to enroll in school. The white man was pale, with brown hair and bloodshot, gray eyes. He appeared to be in his forties, maybe even fifty. Pearl gave me a blissful stare, and then a sly grin while she gripped his arm like he was about to run off. I caught myself gaping at her. I was surprised to see her with another man so soon after Herman Camm.

I suppose I believed she had changed since her days in Jefferson. I guess it is like folks say, "You can't teach ole dogs new tricks . . ."

The train to Petersburg ran several times a day. Some brave folks caught the early train to Petersburg to work and the late train home at night. Most students stayed the entire week and only came home on the weekend. I figured I would come home on Thursday after my class was over. It felt strange that I was carrying this out. That I was doing all of this without the consent of Simon or my momma. I was doing it for me. I wrote a letter to my neighbor Hester, who had chosen to finish college in Washington, about it. She said to do my best to get away from the ways which the white folks had inflicted on coloreds. She said colored folk deserved to be happy too. She had always been the wiser of us two.

Nadine's husband was standing in front of the train when I arrived on the train platform. He glanced over at me, smiled, and threw up his hand and waved. As I started up the steps to the colored car, he called out, "Hey, neighbor, where are you headed?"

Hastily, he walked over to me. I was standing at the last car. Wrong but customary that most colored people sat in the rear cars. "I'm going over to Petersburg for the day," I answered.

The last time I had seen him had been months earlier when he was sitting on the front porch watching Nadine prance back and forth. Nadine grinned every time he tapped her on the rear end. I thought it was a strange way of showing affection, but I would since my husband was never home with me.

There was something dignified about Jessie in a uniform. His mannerisms were serious and professional. Colored folk could never be anything but serious considering that most white people still resented that the slaves had been freed in 1864.

"If you need anything, let me know. I will be in the rear of the last car. I'll look for you when we reach Petersburg." He walked away with his shoulders leaning back and his chest sticking out. The uniform had that effect on most men; it gave them a sense of entitlement. Lord knows, colored men needed something to make them feel special.

"Thank you," I replied, and sat down in a seat beside a middle-aged lady who had her head back and eyes closed. She never mumbled a word when I accidently pushed against her. "Good morning," I said. She didn't even say good morning. She kept her eyes closed and never flinched.

It was early, though; the sunlight had just begun to break. I was also sleepy. The jerks and swerves of the train could wake a dead person, and the rumble was subtly annoying. She was dressed in a formal maid's uniform. My guess was she worked in Petersburg, and probably at some white person's mansion. For a minute, I remembered going with Momma to Mrs. Ferguson's and how she would scrub her clothes clean with her bare hands, and then dry and iron them before returning home. Once she was home, she'd do the same for us. She even made sure Mrs. Ferguson's dinner was warming on the stove and the table set before putting on her hat for the trip home. Mrs. Ferguson was an uppity white woman. I never cared for her, and especially the way she'd look down her finely chiseled nose at the people making her life easier. I doubt she liked me either.

The trip was quick. And when the train screeched as it came to a stop, the lady sitting with me adjusted her hat, picked up the bag in between her legs, and headed to the door.

I arrived in Petersburg about forty minutes

after the train had pulled off from the depot in Richmond. The train made multiple stops along the route picking up people who were either going to Petersburg to work or to Norfolk for an extended stay. All of the riders in my car were colored. The white patrons were in the train up front. Even though they were separated from the coloreds as if we were diseased, I could see them through the train window smiling and talking. As I was getting off the train, Jessie rushed over to assist me down the steps. "I hope to see you again soon," he said, as if he really meant it.

"We will probably see a lot of each other, since I will be going to school down here." He turned and smiled.

"By the way, when will you be back in Richmond? I see your wife and children almost every day sitting on the porch across the street."

He seemed a bit rattled by my comment. A frown seemed to appear immediately above his thick eyebrows. "Nadine is not my wife, and they are not my children."

"I'm sorry. I just thought . . ." He cut me off.

"Don't be. She had the children before we met. I was going to marry her, but she turned out to be a different kind of woman.

She's not the marrying type. Now the children, they are some good kids."

"Sorry to hear that. You take care," I said, in an attempt to end the conversation. I could tell he wanted to talk more. He moved in closer to me and whispered in my ear, "You are a beautiful woman."

I shrugged my shoulders and struggled to release a smile. His manner seemed a bit inappropriate, since I was a married woman. So I said, "See you later," and took off in a rapid stride down the road in the direction of Virginia Normal and Collegiate Institute. When I reached the corner, I turned and glanced back at Jessie. He was still watching me, peering straight at me.

The school was set up the same way the Union school had been. It was a short walk from the train station. Most, if not all, of the students were women. All of them yearning, like me, to teach school. I sat with my legs crossed and poured my heart out to the administrator. She was a serious woman. Had walked down Pennsylvania Avenue in the Women's Suffrage March in 1913, and understood how it was for women and young people of color in America. "Women need a purpose in life. We're not secondhand citizens," Mrs. Middleton said.

"Yes, ma'am," I replied. "I want to help

94

the people around me to learn, so they can dream bigger than the farm."

She was a founding member of a women's organization called Delta Sigma Theta Sorority.

"Being on a farm is somewhere to be proud of living. Most of us come from farms," she added.

"I've always wanted to teach, and I can't wait to get started."

"First, you need to fill out these forms for our records."

She handed me two documents to fill out. As I sat at the desk answering questions, Mrs. Middleton watched me. I felt she was analyzing me, sizing me up. I sat as poised as possible, and tried to be as ladylike as I possibly could. Momma always said appearances were important. In Mrs. Middleton's office were books on everything, from geography to mathematics.

When I turned in the last form with my address and family information on it, she gave me a book to read. She told me to come back in two weeks when classes started. I smiled.

I stopped by a rooming house across from the campus. The colored lady who ran the house told me I could stay there, share a room with another student, if I helped her prepare the food for the other students who had money to pay. I agreed. I had been cooking most of my life anyway.

On the way back to the train station, I realized I had thought about everything but little Robert. How could I go to school with a baby? I didn't know how I would handle it, but I knew there would be a way.

I didn't see Jessie when I boarded the train heading back to Richmond. I was sort of indifferent about seeing him. I wasn't sure why he told me I was beautiful. Was it because he was lonely? Or had he been sincere? It sounded inappropriately good. I hadn't seen my own husband in over a month.

Robert was sitting in Mrs. Hall's lap when I got back home. His jovial eyes gleamed as she bounced him on her knee. He glanced at me, smiled and then reached with both hands for me. He was so charming. My heart filled with love when I saw him, and I wondered how I could go to school and leave my little boy.

"Well, what happened down in Petersburg?"

"I enrolled, Mrs. Hall."

"Good, child. When will you begin?"

"In two weeks."

"Good; now how many days will you be

in Petersburg?"

"I will be there for four days a week. I've got to find someone to look after Robert for me while I'm in school."

"We'll take care of him for you. He's used to us. Let us help you."

"Mrs. Hall, that is too much to ask of you."

"I like having Robert. He is like the child we always wanted. My husband loves him like his own. Besides, you and Simon are like our children too. Now, before you say no, talk to Simon about it. Send him a letter."

"I don't think Simon would want me in school."

"Why not?"

"He thinks I should wait here until his career as a baseball player has taken off."

"It is always about the man." She giggled.

"What do you mean?"

"Honey, this is the twenties. A woman is supposed to be beside her man, behind her man, but never equal. In other words, women are supposed to cook, clean and open their legs when their husbands desire. There is more to life than being a housewife."

"Did you want more, Mrs. Hall?"

"I wanted more, and I had more. I had

my own business. When I met my husband, people couldn't understand our relationship, so I sold the business and we moved here."

"So, you did that for your husband?"

"No, I did it for me. He never asked me to do anything I didn't want to do. We lived amongst a lot of racists. I didn't want to wake up and find my husband hanging from some tree. I moved here because it is safer. I will go anywhere with him. After all these years, we are still in love."

"I hope Simon will understand."

"He will. Besides, you will be done in no time."

"Mrs. Hall, please don't say anything about this to Simon. I want to talk to him first."

"My lips are sealed."

I went up the stairs with Robert on my hip, shaking my head. Simply baffled.

CHAPTER 9

Simon came home just before the evening breeze had begun to stir up the leaves falling on the cool, dry ground, and as the sun descended behind the clouds. After traveling all over the map, going across the border to Washington and Baltimore, and even driving for three days to St. Louis, Missouri, he needed rest. The Colored League was expanding, but for some reason, Simon felt he hadn't found the right team for himself yet.

Every time I saw my husband, my heart started to do a love dance in my chest, pounding for his attention. And this visit was nonetheless the same. A smile wiped across my face at the sight of him. The reason he had chosen to be a ball player had become prevalent in my thoughts. Finally, and for the first time since I'd been in Richmond, I understood how much Simon longed to be on a team; I had that same unshakable desire to teach children how to read. However, I couldn't share my plans with him.

Simon's instincts were sharp, though. He noticed anything odd or awkward whenever he walked into a room, said he had warning senses. It was good, since I didn't pay that much attention to everything going on around me, partially, because I was a young girl taking on a woman's job with little or no guidance. My daily chores took up my time. Each day slipped into the next; the ritual of making feeding bottles at night and fetching hen eggs in the morning, doing laundry, all had me captivated in motherhood and trying to be a wife. Mr. Hall kept the furnace burning through the crisp fall nights. I had never put wood or coal into a furnace. If the Halls had not been downstairs, Robert and I would be cold at night.

Simon picked up one of Robert's pullovers, and opened it up. "Baby, why are Robert's things packed in a bag over here beside the bed?" he asked, and threw his old duffle bag loaded with soiled clothes from red clay and dirt from roaming from second base to catcher beside our bed. For me, It would make sense to find a place on a team and stick to it. Washing his uniforms by hand was more than a chore. I'd have to boil water and get the water hot enough in the tub to tackle the red clay and grass stains. Even a capsule of bleach couldn't remove some of the stains engraved in the knees of his pants. Afterward, my hands were usually tired.

I had been pulling things out of the oak chifferobe the past two days, carefully folding Robert's diapers and the little T-shirts Momma had made for him, into tiny piles. I wanted to leave Mrs. Hall with everything she needed for Robert while I was away. The booties I had knitted would go as well. He didn't have a pair of hard bottom shoes yet. Simon had promised to order them from the Sears catalog for Christmas. With each garment, my hands trembled. I was doing something my momma and husband would say was unfit for a good mother.

"I'm just sorting his things. I'm putting the things Robert has outgrown in a separate bag, to be passed on to somebody who needs things for a little baby," I lied.

"Why would you get rid of them? You can use them when you get pregnant again," he said, removing his soiled clothes from the bag and placing them on the floor.

When I heard him, I bit my lip to keep from swearing. Why in hell would I want to have a baby at this time? He didn't know what it took to raise Robert.

Simon's words pierced my soul. *A baby!* He barely knew what it took to snap beans, slice meat, cook, and wash clothes all with a baby hanging on your hip. When Simon decided to be home with me, and work a paying job in Richmond, I would give him as many children as he wanted. Driving the model T all over the states did not leave much time for raising babies.

"I am not giving away everything, just some things. There's a lady with a little boy down the block."

"You need to keep them for yourself," he demanded.

"All right, Simon, I heard you," I answered.

"We can start tonight," he said.

"I'm not sure a baby is what we need," I answered.

"Why not a baby?" he asked, pulling me close to him. Just the sensation of his breath against the side of my face had me vulnerable. I could have undressed at that moment for him. I didn't, though. Instead, I attempted to explain.

"It's just that you are gone most of the time. I don't want to do it alone again. It is hard enough for Robert and me. We miss you, and since we don't have any kinfolk around us, it is a little lonely. I second-guess myself most of the time because I don't know anything about raising a child."

"Carrie, this is a good neighborhood. Everybody looks out for each other. You will be safe and I know the Halls would be happy to help you, if necessary. Every child wants a sister or brother."

The Halls had already opened their hearts up to Robert and me. They were like godparents to him; at least that is what I prayed they would be. Aside from the occasional visits from Momma, they are all the family he has. They love him so much; they reach for him whenever I go somewhere. Mrs. Hall's blue eyes light up and Mr. Hall seems content with Robert in their possession. He's always bouncing him on his knee like Robert is riding a horse. Mrs. Hall said they always wanted children of their own, but she could never carry a baby to term. Their love for Robert is majestic and pure. I left him with them when I enrolled in school and I planned on leaving him with them for four days a week while I was studying in Petersburg.

"Simon, can we talk about a baby at another time?"

"Having children is natural. Most people don't plan children; they just come. But if you insist, we can talk later. Seems to me now is as good a time as any to add to our family."

After Robert was fast asleep, Simon pulled me into the bedroom. I quickly excused myself to the bathroom, searched in the back of the cabinet for my sponge, and inserted it for birth control.

When I returned, as Simon lay me down on my back, I was confident I wouldn't get pregnant. I had taken the precautions any ambitious woman should take to pursue her own goals. So, when Simon kissed me on the forehead and then deep on the lips, I succumbed. His tongue went deep in my mouth, sampling my fluids. With each kiss, I lost control. I parted my thighs and coaxed his hard manhood into my sweetness. My syrup was flowing like honey from a bee hive. His sting was so inviting, I threw my head back and released myself to him. Simon thrust and thrust on me like a machine. I loved every moment, especially because I had my little secret weapon — the sponge.

Simon whispered, "I miss you, girl."

I murmured back, "I miss you, too."

I gripped his back and pulled him close to me. Simon loved it.

"I love you, girl," he whispered.

While Simon slept, I went into the bathroom, removed the sponge, and put it back in my special place.

The fall was rapidly moving in. The mornings were damp and chilly. The trees barren, the leaves blanketing the ground like a tapestry bed quilt. Simon took advantage of the cool weather, and tossed the thick quilt on the foot of the bed. He woke up early the next morning. He started out by gathering the hens' eggs and cleaning out the feathers and dirt in the chicken coop. He threw sawdust on the floor and patched up places where the winter wind chill could seep through and disturb the chickens. Afterward, he helped me hang out the clothes on the line in the backyard. For a while, I felt like he was going to stay. But, I knew better.

That afternoon, when I heard her knuckles tapping on the door, I cringed. Nadine knew how to rattle my nerves. She knocked for a few minutes before Simon opened the door.

"Come in," he said.

Nadine came in smiling.

"I thought I'd pay you two a visit."

"Please sit down," Simon said.

She came in the parlor and sat directly across from Simon in the high-back chair.

I watched the way she sashayed into the house, and how she purposely sat directly in front of my husband. What was more sickening than her being there was how she sat with her thighs parted and pulled her dress up above her knees when she crossed her legs. Nadine was a deliberate woman. One who could rouse up even the mildest of temperaments. My nerves were so frayed that I wanted to jump out of my chair and choke her until she recognized I was sick of her.

"Nadine, I saw your husband the other day."

Her eyes shifted. "Where did you see him?" I could tell I had made her nervous when she began to play with her hands, rubbing them as if she had experienced a chill.

"In the neighborhood."

"Wonder why he was around here. I thought he was on the train somewhere."

"This is where he lives."

"How often does he come home?" Simon asked.

"Well, we are sort of separated."

"Sorry to hear about your marriage."

"He didn't know how to handle a woman like me," she said, peering at Simon in a seductive way.

"He seems to be a nice man," I said.

"He couldn't take care of me. I need me a big strong man like Simon."

"How are your children handling all of this?" Simon asked, ignoring what she had implied.

"They didn't like him anyway. He wasn't their daddy."

Simon was not looking in the direction of Nadine. He was staring at me, as if there was something I should have been doing. Finally, I said it. "Nadine, we were about to go out."

"I just wanted to say hello to Simon. I miss you every time you come home. I told your wife to tell you hello the last time you came home."

Simon narrowed his eyes, and glanced over at me.

I didn't say a word, but I watched Nadine give my husband a peep at her private area when she uncrossed her legs to leave.

I walked her to the door.

"Next time, Nadine, stay at home."

"What?"

"You heard me!"

CHAPTER 10

Simon stayed for a full week. He seemed a little different about his stay. He was not as anxious to leave and get back on the road. While he was home, there was good news about the newly formed Colored League had open dialogue with Rube Foster and others to form the Eastern Colored Baseball League. The league would have protection from the invasion of the larger white teams. The formation of organized teams with paid memberships had opened doors to more games and involvement from teams like the Kansas City Monarchs and Baltimore Black Barons. Simon loved the news, and felt warm about the opportunity to join a team permanently.

All week, I'd watch Nadine sitting on the porch in the cool weather waiting for my husband to come outside. And when she'd see him, she would yell, "Hey, Simon, it is going to be a good day today."

He'd wave and continue with what he was doing.

It was the middle of the week, and the fall wind had been strong, so brisk it chilled your cheeks. The last of the leaves were floating to the ground, and most of the trees were barren. Nadine had been sitting on her porch all morning with a winter coat and hat on waiting for Simon to come out of the apartment. She had a weird obsession with him. When Simon started to the corner store, she came off the porch, ran to catch up with him, and walked with him to the store.

I watched them go out of sight to the store. It wasn't long before Nadine and Simon appeared between the two pine trees and Simon came into the house.

Before he could unpack the brown paper bag, I wanted to know what had happened.

"Why did Nadine follow you up the street?"

"I don't know, Carrie. She seems to need a lot of attention."

"Has she forgotten that you are married?"

He stopped unpacking the milk and sugar he'd gone for and looked at me.

"I don't want that woman. She is out of her mind."

"Why didn't you say something to her?

Why did you let her tag along? She went with you to the store, Simon."

"She seems to do a lot of things she shouldn't. She must be lonely. She wants her husband."

"Simon, did she tell you that? Or are you thinking for her?"

"No, she didn't say anything about her husband. She bought some milk."

"What she is doing is wrong."

"I agree with you. I can't tell a grown woman how to act. I just know she is not my type."

"Did she say something to you?"

"She was saying a lot of stuff. I really wasn't listening to that woman. I was not interested," he said, shaking his head.

"I will never trust her. She wants you, and you are my husband."

"It takes two people for something to happen. I am not interested in Nadine. She is a woman across the street. Let's not waste our time together worrying about her. We have got too many other things to talk about."

"I want to know what she said."

"It is not important. You are my wife."

"Now you see why she could never be my friend. She's a slut."

"Carrie, we are going out tonight. Let me

110

do something special for you."

A smile rolled across my face.

"Where are we going?"

"We are going to see Ms. Pearl Brown."

Pearl was a superstar wherever she traveled; at least she acted like one. People at home in Jefferson said she was a big put-on — full of herself. It amazed me how little people from the country really knew. I couldn't wait to go back to the club. Watching the patrons come in and out was as much excitement for me as listening to Pearl's sultry and seductive voice turn on the men. I envisioned Pearl entertaining on many levels, especially after seeing her with a white man. The businesses and community folk all gathered there just like we did in Jefferson at the church. The city had more than one place to fellowship and I liked the idea of places where I wouldn't be judged.

The evening didn't roll in fast enough. I couldn't wait to dress up, and put a little lipstick on my lips. Simon seemed to enjoy places like the club. I wondered if, while he was on the road, he went to places like that often. My guess is, he did.

"I can't wait to see Ms. Pearl singing again."

"I noticed how much you enjoyed it the

last time we were there."

"She has a beautiful voice, and everyone seems to love her." I paused. "You know, I saw Ms. Pearl coming out of the Jefferson Hotel with a white man."

"Carrie, you don't understand how the world is. People are always watching and judging you. Pearl should be careful. Her reputation is what she'll have left when her singing voice is raspy and her career is on the downfall."

"Is it the same way you feel about base-ball?"

"In a way, I suppose. Most people are not concerned about an athlete's personal life. They just want him to perform physically when he is on the field."

"Does it mean you can do wrong, and not be held accountable for it?"

"No, but sports players are a little differ-ent."

"Shouldn't we all watch our behavior, especially in public?"

"Yeah, we should.

"Are you about ready? I am driving to-night."

"I am. I want to see if everything looks good. I can't wait to see Mrs. Walker again too."

He chuckled.

"I can't believe my country little wife is so excited about the city. I am so glad you are leaving the Jefferson ways behind."

"You used to like my ways."

"I still do. I'm country too. I am happy you are not judging the people at the club. People from our hometown might not like me taking you to a nightclub."

"I don't care what they like," Carrie commented.

"Me either. Hurry up so we can take Robert downstairs to Mrs. Hall."

"I hope I am not leaning on her too much."

"She loves little Robert, and her husband loves him being with them."

"Who would have thought a white woman would take to a colored child?" Carrie said.

"She's different. She is family like any colored person. She has given up a lot to be married to a colored man. She is comfortable in this community. They are the best neighbors anybody could have."

"She's like my best friend."

"Isn't she too old for that?"

"No, she is a friend. Are you still trying to get me to talk to Nadine?"

"Not anymore."

"Nadine is not a friend, Simon. She is the

opposite. Even Momma told me to watch her."

"Well, then you should," he said, shaking his head. "You ready?"

I stood in front of the chifferobe mirror, meticulously twisting my hair with my fingers, turning my curls under into a bob.

"Come on; let's go," Simon anxiously said, grinning.

I picked up Robert and headed for the door. Simon grabbed his bottle and followed close behind me.

As we climbed into the Model T Ford, Nadine came out the house bouncing with each stride.

"Hi, Simon!"

He ignored her. So did I and I looked in the opposite direction.

We got in the car and drove the four blocks to the club on the corner of Adams Street. The crowd was already lining up to enter. Ladies and gentlemen were patiently waiting to get into the club and catch a glimpse of the community celebrities. Simon and I parked across the street behind a brand-new Studebaker and joined the already restless crowd in line. It appeared the whole community had come out for Pearl Brown. There were several white people patiently waiting as well. One of the men

114

resembled the man I'd seen Pearl holding hands with as they left the Jefferson Hotel. Once inside, we found a seat up front near the stage. The first time we were here, we sat in the middle.

"Can we sit up front?" I begged like a little child. "The closer to the action, the better . . ."

We located a table on the right side of the stage, closer to the entrance and bar.

The tables were filling up fast. There were a few wooden stools around the outskirts, in case the seats were all taken. On this fall evening, everyone was coming out.

Shortly after we were seated, a lady came over to our table. I had never seen her before. She was brown and stout, with an appealing smile.

"Hi, Simon; it is good to see you again," she said, smiling seductively at my husband.

"Hi," he said, nodding.

"I didn't know you lived in Richmond," she commented in a puzzled tone of voice.

She ignored me and continued gazing at Simon. Simon twiddled his fingers together, like he was nervous about something.

"Yes, I do. This is my wife, Carrie." He abruptly stopped the conversation and glanced over at me.

"Oh, hi," she said.

I smiled.

A frown rolled across her lips.

"I guess I'd better take a seat," she said and walked off as if her feelings had been hurt.

Simon didn't say anything and neither did I. I wondered who that lady could be to Simon. She seemed to disappear into the crowd.

Mrs. Walker strutted in the door wearing a pink satin dress and gloves, a mink stole on her arm. Her partner, a dark stately fellow in a navy suit and bow tie escorted her to a reserved table in the front which was centered in front of the stage. I couldn't keep my eyes off her. She was elegant and powerful. She held her head up high, and her shoulders squared. Her demeanor was of leadership and control. A nod and a smile was her way of acknowledging the people in the crowd waving excitedly at her. I sat still, my eyes roving from place to place, trying not to miss anything.

Everyone seemed to loosen up at places like the nightclub. After everyone had had a drink of liquor, the atmosphere started to change. Stiff faces softened and laughter emerged throughout the room. Simon kept smiling at me as if he were dazzled by something I had done. Maybe it was because

I didn't ask about the lady who'd abruptly vanished into the crowd.

"Here she comes," I said.

Ms. Pearl waltzed in with Willie on her arm. Willie was smiling from ear to ear. She had on a royal-blue dress, which glimmered with the lights. It was tight-fitting and hugged her hips with an unyielding grip.

She sauntered up to the stage to thunderous applause from the patrons. With an interlude of humming, she began to belt out the words. Everyone stood on their feet. Simon and I stood too. After a few seconds, we all sat down and listened to her and the band fill the room with soft music that had everyone swaying their heads. Willie stood on the side and watched with the inflated chest of a proud man. Simon casually waved to him, and he smiled in return.

"She is singing tonight, baby," Simon whispered in my ear.

"She is better than she was last time."

Simon reached over and took my hand in his. I grinned, and squeezed his fingers.

The mood was so relaxed, a few patrons stood around at their tables slow-dancing cheek to cheek.

The white man I had seen with Pearl stood right behind Willie. It was as if Pearl was singing to him too. Who could tell?

Ms. Pearl continued singing and then shifted her eyes to the other side of the room. It was strange to me, since it was obvious Willie was enjoying her gazing at him from the stage.

All of a sudden, there was a large pop, and several thereafter. I panicked.

The crowd started screaming. Ms. Pearl rushed off the stage, her band members protecting her. Simon grabbed me and pulled me to the cold floor. The crowd was frantic. One lady tripped to the ground. She grabbed her ankle. "Please help me," she said and a large man came to her rescue. He lay on top of her, and told her to stay down. We stayed under the table until the shots stopped. Afterward, Simon and I raised up off the floor. The rest of the crowd did the same. He took my hand and coaxed me through the hysterical crowd that was scrambling and pushing toward the front door.

My heart was thumping, my chest heaving up and down. Everybody had incredulous looks on their faces. It was a horrid scene. People stood around watching. Pearl was slumped over a body crying, "Oh, Lawd; oh, Lawd!"

"Who is that on the floor?!" someone

yelled, as we pressed toward the front entrance.

"It is Willie Brown!" another replied.

"Who?" the voices echoed.

CHAPTER 11

As I turned to look behind us as we traveled west out of the city past the large sign advertising the Nehi Grape, I became a little concerned. The further away we drove from the city, the warmer I became. Beads of sweat trickled down the sides of my hairline. As we passed the last house alongside the road and then a two-lane highway became a narrow road, I was reminded Jefferson County was closer than I needed it to be.

"You all right?" Simon asked, tapping my thigh.

"I'll be all right directly," I said, swallowing.

"What do you mean by that?"

"I wasn't planning on going home so soon. For some reason, I wanted Jefferson County to be a memory only," I said.

Simon reached for my hand. "You've got family there. Try to put all of that stuff behind you."

"I don't know how some of the townsfolk are going to treat me."

"Most people are good."

"Well, not to me."

"Believe me, I am not going to let anything happen to you."

"I know."

The ride lasted only two hours. We traveled right past the fueling station and then onto a dusty two-lane road past Mrs. Ferguson's farm. The closer we came to the big white mansion with large columns on the outside overlooking a lawn with neatly trimmed shrubbery, the more old memories were ignited, mainly of Mrs. Ferguson treating my momma as if she were less than her dog, which she cared for better than any human being. Many days when Momma forced me to go with her to the house, Mrs. Ferguson, in bright red lipstick, would walk behind Momma like a shadow giving out orders. "Mae Lou, now clean the mantel good today. I am inviting guests over. I don't want them to feel I have a poor maid," and Momma would only say, "Yes, ma'am." Her ruby-red lips spat condescending words to my momma, who always sought to please and be loyal to the insulting Southern Belle.

We pulled into Momma's yard just before the last sun cloud slithered out of sight. The sky was a beautiful burnt-orange and the air fresh. There was a dim light glaring from the kitchen window, and with it spawned memories of the nights my brothers and I stayed up way past midnight playing dominoes by candlelight. At times we strained our eyes so much they were bloodshot. Tonight I knew it was Momma either baking for the next day or reading her Bible as she was known for doing before retiring to bed.

Little Robert had slept most of the trip on a quilt thrown across the backseat. He managed to sleep soundly despite all the bumps on the dirt road, and he had only cried once, and that was when he woke and didn't see me. After he heard my voice in the front seat of the car, he closed his eyes and went back to sleep. I'm sure the fresh country air helped to put him to sleep.

Nightfall was approaching. Living in the country could be special and mesmerizing when you gazed up in the sky and the stars stared down brightly from above. They seemed close enough to touch. There are other times when it was cloudy and not a gleam from the sky, when it was a gloomy place to live until the rooster crows at the break of dawn.

Simon got Robert and I carried his bag.

With each step to the front door, I inhaled deep breaths. I was going home. A place I really did not want to be.

We knocked on the door, and went in. Like most people in the country, the latch was not on the door. I heard Momma yell from the kitchen, "Who is that?"

"It is me, Momma."

"Lord, why you didn't let me know you was coming? I would have cooked a decent meal."

"Don't worry about us."

"Y'all come on in. It is so nice to see y'all."

"I hope we didn't scare you," Simon said.

"No, I leave the door open sometimes for Carl. I usually lock it before turning in for the night. Y'all want something to eat. I got a couple of pieces of fried chicken and a few collards left on the stove."

"I am a little hungry," Simon answered.

Momma lifted Robert right out of my arms. She put him on her hip and he grabbed a hold of her dress. She didn't waver. She went to the stove and started dumping forkfuls of collards and chicken on to plates. Simon and I sat waiting to be served, since she insisted on feeding us. Little Robert smiled and held tight as Momma went back and forth from the table to the stove. Momma should have put him down, but she didn't. It was time for him to start walking. Momma said I walked at nine months and boys sometimes took a little longer to take the first step. Robert was very comfortable being held. I wasn't sure if he couldn't do it, or decided not to walk at that moment.

After Momma had fixed a small saucer of gravy and a biscuit to feed Robert, she sat down. Simon started by asking Momma about herself.

"I'm doing well. I spend my days keeping busy. I get up with the chickens and go to bed when the sun goes behind the clouds."

Little Robert smacked his mouth as Momma shoved pieces of biscuits soaked in gravy into his mouth. He loved it, and grunted several times because Momma wasn't feeding him fast enough.

"I'm glad things are working out around here."

"Yes, indeed, they are working out."

"Carl get over here often?"

"Lawd, that boy is over here almost every day."

"Carrie, you all right?" Simon asked me.

"I'm just enjoying Momma's cooking."

"Ain't it a shame what happened to poor Willie up yonder. I tell you that girl Pearl ain't nothing but trouble."

Momma was different since I was no longer in her house. She used to be tight-lipped and unattached. Now she was talking to us like she did to Mr. Camm. She even gazed at us in our faces. She was different now. She seemed free. She had been delivered from whatever had been holding her captive. I wondered if it had been Papa, Mr. Camm, or her children.

"We wanted to pay our respects to Willie, so we drove home."

"Pearl is just trouble, I tell you. He was happy being with her. He done fought in the army for us and lived; now he is dead because of Pearl."

"Momma, nobody really knows what happened," I said.

"People knows."

"Ms. Pearl was on the stage singing when it happened. I'm not sure she had anything to do with the shooting."

"Folks say the white man who shot him is her ole man. She can't keep her hands to herself to save her life. She is a trouble-maker. I know my life would have been better if she had not come to town."

I cringed when she made that conviction. I couldn't keep quiet.

"Momma, Mr. Camm was not a good person. Ms. Pearl didn't make him do the

125

things he did. He did them all by himself. Ms. Pearl was a victim too."

"Now there you go taking up for her. She is not a decent lady. I'll bet she has spent the best part of her adult life causing pain for married and single women alike. Pearl don't care about nobody but Pearl Brown."

"I don't want to rush to judgment, Momma."

"She parades her ways in front of people. She never even stops to say I'm sorry. A woman ain't got no business fooling around."

I bit my tongue. I squirmed and inhaled to keep from opening my mouth. It was no secret Momma knew Camm before Papa passed. I'd often wondered where she met him. She and Betsy would go to Washington, D.C. occasionally and when she came back, she would have a sly smile all over her face.

"Momma," Simon said, "Ms. Pearl may not feel she is hurting anybody."

Momma put Robert across her shoulder. He had been fighting sleep. "I'm not going to say what she knows, but it don t take too much to see she is not a person you want to be around. Now she done got two men killed. What on earth could be next?"

Momma was not going to give Ms. Pearl the benefit of doubt. In her mind, the mention of the name Pearl was trouble; folks in Jefferson left the room and ducked their heads. She had that effect on some of the frightened, confined residents. It was so troubling for Momma that frown lines spread horizontally across her forehead. We finished eating and I washed the dishes like I had always done, putting them on the drain board to air-dry. Momma went to bed humming one of her spirituals, her voice as raspy as a tobacco-smoking man. She seemed happy. She put Robert in the bed beside her, and he glanced up at her and smiled, his little gums shining with spit. Simon and I slept in my old room. The sky was so black, and the moon neon bright. I fell asleep in Simon's arms peering at the moon.

The next day we got up early. I went outside to the chicken coop and gathered the eggs. Momma sat in the kitchen chair watching me through the window. When I came back, she reached for the eggs and began breaking them into hot grease left from frying fatback. The aroma filled up the kitchen, and immediately my tongue started to salivate. It was almost like old times, until she stopped and turned around with a serious stare in her eyes.

"You know you really have grown up, Carrie."

I smiled. "Yes, ma'am."

"Try to enjoy your life. Don't live it for nobody but yourself and the good Lawd."

"I will, Momma. Don't worry," I assured her, surprised by her comment.

"I ain't worried. I just want better for you. Girls don't supposed to live hard," she said.

"Momma, I live a good life."

"Good!" she murmured. "Good."

All I could think about was that we were here for yet another funeral. It hadn't been a year since Mr. Camm had been murdered, and now we were going back to the same church where my Momma and Papa had taken us to fellowship with God and the neighbors. Carl came over as Momma was getting ready to serve breakfast.

He saw me, grabbed me up out of the chair and draped his long arms around me. "I'm so glad to see you, Sis. I thought you weren't ever gonna come home. People leave from around here and never come back," he said, studying me hard.

I blushed. "You know I will always come home," I said, still in his embrace. Then I took a seat at the table.

"I sure miss you. Mary and I done decided to start a family. It is lonesome up around here without children. Little Robert can come down and spend the summer with us when he is old enough to use the outhouse."

"He is growing fast. I can't wait to know my nieces and nephews. I'm so glad you decided to start a family," I said, smiling and wishing they already had children.

"You know folks still talking about Mr. Camm. Now with Willie gone, I'm sure the sheriff is going to come back around here."

"We don't have anything to do with Camm."

"I know, but his brother come through here a time ago and he's got the sheriff all roused up and ready to hang somebody."

"The sheriff don't care about coloreds," I said.

"The sheriff promised his brother he'd look into finding his killer. But you know white folks don't care if one of us gets killed. They still haven't found the person who murdered James Sanders. I'll bet it was one them white boys dressed in sheets."

"You are right. The sheriff is not going to find out anything. Besides, no one trusts white folks around here enough to open their mouths."

"Camm was not right. He hurt too many people," Simon commented.

"He deserved everything he got," Carl said.

"Shut your mouth, boy. That ain't no way

129

to talk about the dead," Momma said in a frustrated voice.

Carl looked at me and shook his head. I lowered my head.

Simon inhaled and then said, "Momma, you know he did hurt a lot of people. He even hurt you."

I could tell she didn't like what he said. Her eyes rolled around in her head, and she took a deep breath.

"Well, no matter what he done, he is still a child of the Lord's," she replied.

Nobody said another word. It was like her words had a certain biblical meaning even though not one of us felt sorry for the bastard.

"This is gonna be another sad funeral. The boy just got home from the army and now this. He never had a chance." Momma shook her head.

"I didn't know him too well, but he seemed to be a good man," Simon said.

"Anybody who can put up with that Pearl Brown is a good man. She seems to always come out smelling like a rose, after getting men murdered."

Carl mumbled, "Momma, I can tell you don't have any love for her."

"Seem to me the sheriff needs to talk to her," Momma said, and filled her cup up with coffee.

None of us said anything.

We arrived at the church around 12:30. Willie's body was already dressed and lying out in the front of the church. He had on his turtle shell-colored army uniform, and he looked like he was finally at peace. His hat was lying across his chest. Ms. Pearl was standing at the foot of his casket when we came into the church. Her hat with a black veil shadowing her face was the first thing I noticed. She had on black from head to toe. She even used a black, silk handkerchief wiping tears no one could see behind the veil.

Momma grunted at the sight of her. We took a seat toward the back of the church. She said, "The front seats are for the family."

The church started to fill up fast. Funerals were like family reunions. Country people sadly searched for any opportunity to fellowship with the community. The town gossipers were also welcomed, since no matter how many people looked down their noses at their wise talk, all ears were tuned in.

Ms. Pearl relished the attention of the community. The men boldly walked up to her, shook her hand, and patted her on the back. Simon even walked up to her and waited for his turn to shake her hand. Momma and I just watched, and at times Momma shook her head. A few of Willie's army friends also came all dressed up in army dress uniforms. I couldn't help thinking about the night he was shot. The white man who did the shooting, what was he really to Ms. Pearl? Would he show up?

"I wish they would get started," Momma said, "Pearl need to take a seat. She done got enough attention."

Before taking a look at poor Willie lying stiff on his back in the casket, most of the people walked straight up to Ms. Pearl. It was like she had given a show and was receiving guests. I could see her lips moving, and an occasional smile at some of the comments; she seemed to be taking his passing with stride.

After the church was full, a little after 1 p.m., the reverend, with his Bible in his hand, took his place at the pulpit. He started with a scripture, and then he began to preach. In a few minutes, he was jumping and hollering; he almost lost his balance and I imagined him tumbling into the opened casket. One of the deacons caught him before he hit the floor. They helped him up and he continued with his sermon, never missing a beat. I knew if Willie could be awakened, he would certainly sit up with all the noise. The reverend was loud and boisterous. At one time, I discreetly put my hands over my ears. He was proclaiming hallelujah and speaking in tongues, shouting so much no one could understand a word he was saying.

"This is a shame," Momma whispered. "All that shouting is not necessary. I wonder if he is shouting for Pearl's attention."

"Momma, I think he is just preaching," I whispered.

"He needs to get on with it." She grunted and rolled her eyes.

I peered across the room at Ginny who was sitting on the side of us. She turned to look at me when the reverend almost slipped off the pulpit. As Carl and another deacon stepped in to catch him when he stumbled, Ginny raised her eyebrows, frowned and shook her head. A couple of other members lowered their heads and attempted to wipe off their smiles. I wanted to laugh myself, but remembered the inappropriateness of laughing at the good reverend.

Willie was buried in the back of the church. After watching the deacons throw dirt on the casket, we headed back to the front of the church. I was coming around the corner of the church yard when the sheriff hastily walked over to me swinging his arms erratically.

"I see you made it back here . . . been waiting to catch you in Jefferson. I hope you don't know about this murder."

"No, sir, I don't," I answered.

He was chewing snuff, his red jaw stuffed with it. Bobby, the sheriff, was not a bad-looking man, but he was anal. And it made most people dislike him.

Bobby walked off as quickly as he had appeared.

CHAPTER 12

"I'm going with y'all back to the house," Ginny said. "That Bobby done got in Carrie's face way too many times. I've got to remind that boy coloreds have sense too."

Ginny climbed into the car, poking her cane in first and stuffing herself between Momma and Robert. She insisted she wanted to be there when Bobby stopped by. She had been Bobby's nanny as a child, and felt she could handle him and keep him honest. "Most of them white boys don't care about coloreds. Bobby don't neither, 'til I remind 'em of my tittie being in his mouth. He gets quiet then, and leaves me alone. You see, he don't want nobody to know. I remember many nights he fell sound to sleep with my nipple in his mouth." Every time she told the story, I nearly upchucked at the thought.

We all sat around the kitchen table talking about the day. Although I was nervous about talking to Bobby, the conversation at the table kept my interest.

"Lawd knows Pearl ought to be 'shamed of herself. She done got in the car with a white man right in front of the peoples at the church," Momma commented.

"They say he killed Willie too," Ginny said, shaking her head in disgust.

"Now you know he should be behind bars. But ya see Willie's a colored boy. White boys don't get charged when they kill us. Besides, Pearl ain't got no business with that man," Momma stressed.

"They say Willie threatened the man," Simon interjected.

"That damn Pearl is always causing problems. I can't wait for somebody to pull her to the side and give her a piece of their mind. I ought to do it myself," Ginny said.

"Aunt Ginny, she hasn't done anything to you."

"She don't have to do anything to me, but if she mess with my family, she done messed with me. She done caused enough uproar for the whole damn town."

"We should all try to put Pearl and all the rest of them behind us and move forward," Simon said. "The people around here will not let things go. They are stuck in the past."

"If only Bobby would let this thing rest,"

Momma remarked, standing at the stove, wiping her hands on her starched apron.

"Now, Simon, I'm gonna need you to take me home after Bobby come," Ginny commanded.

"I will, Aunt Ginny," Simon answered.

"But I ain't going nowhere until he come down here. You know Bobby can be nasty like his daddy. He ain't like coloreds too much. He don't mind you feeding 'em and caring for 'em, but he couldn't stand us any more than that. His momma was nice, though. She came from peoples with money — knew how to treat folk."

"Does anybody want a slice of cake?" Momma asked.

"I'll have a slice, Mae Lou, with some buttermilk, if you got some cold," Ginny requested.

Momma sliced a piece of chocolate cake and poured Ginny a glass of milk.

Simon and I tried to be cool, but both of us were bothered by the sheriff's visit. Simon had a dark, serious stare in his eyes, and kept wiping sweat dripping from his forehead. He had swiped his face several times with a handkerchief. And all the while we were sitting at the kitchen table being amused by Ginny and her comments about raising white children for people who had little love for the caretaker, we had locked hands. My hands were gluey with moisture from rattled nerves. Neither of us knew what to expect. Momma had warned me when she visited about the sheriff opening up Mr. Camm's case, all of it unusual for Jefferson, since most times no one cared about the concerns and troubles of the colored people. We were like the ants; we worked and it was all we did. Our emotions were of no value. I suppose it all started with slavery.

Around five p.m., somebody knocked on the door. It was a steady, hard knock, one which would wake up anybody sleeping. It was the kind of knock all of us knew, even me. Before we opened the door, Momma whispered, "Don't offer no answers on your own. Only answer, yes, sir or no, sir."

"I will."

Bobby sighed at the sight of Ginny sitting at the kitchen table. "Now, Ginny, what are you doing over here?" he said, staring at her with regret.

Ginny had a quick and fierce tongue when necessary. "Well, the law ain't never said folks couldn't visit, Bobby."

"You right, Ginny. I was just askin'," he answered, and backed down.

"This is my family. I thought today was as

138

good as any to pay them a visit. Why are you 'round c'here?"

"Carrie, could you step in the front room for a few questions?"

"Yes, sir," I sputtered, and Momma cut her eyes at me.

I got up, patted down the pleats in my dress and went into the front room. Simon followed close behind me. "Now, you need to go on back. I need to talk to her alone," Bobby said to Simon.

Simon stopped in his tracks and held his hand out. "No problem, sheriff." Simon turned and walked back toward the kitchen, where Ginny and Momma were sitting so still. I knew they were straining to hear the conversation.

I sat down in the paisley, high-back chair my Papa always sat in. Bobby stood in front of me, his hand resting on his pistol. It was an intimidating pose. He cleared his throat. "Now don't be nervous, Carrie. I just got a few questions to ask you," he said in a long Southern drawl.

"Yes, sir."

"Now what was your relationship with Herman Camm?"

"He was my stepfather." I answered, paying close attention to the hand he held on his pistol.

"Did you have a good relationship with him?"

"No, sir."

"Why you didn't have a good relationship with him?"

"I just didn't. I was still mourning my papa when he married Momma."

"Did he do anything to you?"

"Like what, sir?"

"Did he touch you in the wrong places?"

"Why are you asking me, Sheriff?"

"I am the one asking questions here. Gal, you answer them."

"He touched me once."

"Did you hate him?"

"I don't know."

"Did you get mad when he touched you?"

"Yes, sir, I did."

"Did you want to kill 'em?"

"No, I never wanted to kill anyone. I wanted him to leave our house."

"Did you sneak out the house and go looking for him on Christmas?"

"No, sir."

"Did you kill 'em?"

I started to tear up. "No, I would never kill anyone. I did not like him, though."

"I hope you ain't lying to me, 'cause I ain't got time to be playing with no nigga, I mean, colored killer."

140

Bobby quickly caught himself.

"I'm not lying, sir. I didn't want him dead."

Before Bobby could say another word, Ginny had come down the hall. When he saw her, he paused and threw up his hands. "Ginny, now I asked you to stay in the goddamn kitchen."

"I asked you to not hurt my kinfolk. This is my niece. She crying."

"I didn't make her cry. She doing it on her own."

"I heard her tell you she didn't do nothing to Camm. You know he had a lot of enemies, Bobby. Now, you need to gwon."

"Ginny, if I didn't know you, I'd lock you up for messing with my investigation."

"I ain't messed with no damn 'vestigation. I want to help you. She didn't kill 'em."

Bobby adjusted his holster. Then he said, "I guess you telling the truth."

"Yes, sir, I am."

"You better not be lying to me or I will lock your colored butt up."

He started toward the front door and stopped. "Ginny, you need a ride home?"

"Naw, you gwon. I'll get home directly."

Bobby changed his entire disposition when Ginny walked in the room. His approach was less intensive. It was like he had some compassion, at least for Ginny. She knew it, and used her influence to get him to stop his nonsense interrogation of me.

"Y'all folks have a good evening," Bobby said, tilting his hat, before walking out the door.

Ginny put her arm around my shoulder. We walked back into the kitchen. Simon, Carl and Momma all had concerned faces. Little Robert had even been quiet in Momma's arms.

"I'm so glad he is gone," I said.

"You all right, Carrie?" Simon asked.

"He made me nervous. I am so tired of hearing Mr. Camm's name."

"All of us are tired," Carl reiterated.

This was the first time I had seen Carl so flustered; his round eyes were glaring. He had always appeared relaxed about most things, and he reminded me of my papa. My papa had a mild spirit. Today Carl seemed unsure and overly concerned for someone who had nothing to do with the crime. He moved without control. He got up from the chair, gazed out at the clouds and sat back down. Beads of sweat rolled down his temples. Even Ginny recognized it. "Carl, are you all right?"

"Yes, ma'am. I didn't know what to expect from a white sheriff. You know white people

142

do not like us."

"Yo sista is the one he wanted to talk to, not you," she said. "Now you calm down."

Momma was silent. Her beautiful eyes narrowed, and she bit her lip. Carl was shaking his leg relentlessly up and down. It was something he'd do whenever he was nervous. I did it too. Momma and Carl seemed drained by the visit even more than I was, even though I had puffy eyes from crying. At that moment, I wondered who really was the guilty one.

After Bobby was out of sight, we all sat around the table talking about the funeral. None of us brought up Mr. Camm. We all discussed the amount of people who came out to show Willie respect, and pretended Bobby was never there.

"Any colored man who has served in the wa' ought to be honored," Ginny said. "Colored men don't get no respect. I'm sho glad the peoples came out for Willie."

"You right; so many coloreds go unnoticed," Momma said.

"What got under my skin was Pearl Brown. She left with a white man in a new, shiny black Studebaker . . . one of them just like Mr. Ferguson drive," Carl said.

Simon shook his head. "He's the man accused of killing Willie."

"Now that is a damn shame," Ginny said.

"I told ya'll that woman is trouble," Momma reminded us.

"Yes, she is something else. She is the devil, I tell you, the devil."

Then I said, "We don't know what really happened. Only Ms. Pearl can tell us, and the white man."

"The devil, I tell you. It ain't nothing but the devil," Momma added.

Nobody really knew Pearl Brown. We knew the show girl, the entertainer, the singer, yet none of us could relate to her. Nobody had actually had more than a passing conversation with her. We all were on the outside gazing in, wondering what her life was about. We all had formulated opinions, but nobody could say much. Just like the murder of Herman Camm, it was also a mystery. Jefferson County had more to gossip about now, than when I'd left. All I knew was getting out of Jefferson County again would be on the top of my list of things to do and as soon as possible.

CHAPTER 13

Simon drove the speed limit and more trying to get us out of Jefferson, and I was elated when we sped past the Ferguson house on our way back to 460, a two-lane highway leading back to Richmond. I hoped Bobby was done on his venture to find a killer, something which he really didn't care about, only saw it as a way to harass colored folks. I was a better sheriff than him; I thought I knew who killed the monster.

"I don't like that cracker," Simon said as we passed the Fergusons' mansion. Although I would never say it out loud, I hated Mrs. Ferguson, too, for the way she looked down her pointed nose at my momma. I didn't like my momma being directed to the back door instead of the front door when she came to clean.

"Simon, I've never heard you call someone out of their name before."

"Bobby brings out the worst in everybody.

He don't like coloreds and will do anything to bring them down."

"Who do you think killed Camm, Simon?" I asked, almost knowing the answer.

"I don't know, and don't give a damn," he said, and I watched a frown ripple across his forehead.

"You all right?" I asked.

Simon inhaled and said, "He did a lot of things to a lot of people around Jefferson. He wanted to die. He was ordering his own death sentence."

"Nobody wants to die."

"Carrie, he hurt you, your momma and Pearl. He was a gambler, a drunk and a careless bastard. He set his own self up. I just can't feel sorry for him."

"Nobody has the right to take a life," I argued, even though I knew Camm didn't care about nobody.

"Right, unless you don't care about living. So to me he got exactly what he deserved," Simon said, without blinking an eye.

"When will we be able to put this behind us?"

"Now, we will. That sheriff questioned you, and forgot about me. I could have killed him myself."

When he made the comment, I stared at him. The serious glare that was in his eyes

146

was far too cold for the Simon I loved.

"You couldn't have killed him. There is no way you did it."

Simon didn't comment. He just kept his eyes steady on the road, grinding his teeth like a madman.

I was beginning to believe there were more things about my husband I knew little about. I still remembered the lady in the club and how she had approached Simon. I wonder where they had met, and why he didn't take the time to explain her presence. Eventually, it would all come out. I prayed it was something I could understand.

The winds had picked up and we'd weathered the pitter-patter of thunderous rain most of the way home. Even though the red country dirt had splashed all over Simon's Ford. He had a lot of pride in that car. He said he'd bought it from a white man in Baltimore, Maryland. The man was feeling kind of terrible about the way he'd treated his own colored children, so when he was full of liquor, he decided to sell Simon his car for next to nothing. Simon bought the car, and the white man freed his soul. Now both of them were happy. "Soon the rain ends, I'm gonna clean my tires off. A man can't drive around with dirt on his vehicle. I don't want the folks to say we don't deserve it."

"I'm tired of worrying about people. I just want things to be right for us."

Simon tapped me on the thigh. "We gonna be all right."

We pulled into Richmond just as the rain stopped. The only sign left was a beautiful fall rainbow. Robert slept the entire trip back. I missed Momma and Ginny already, although the town, I could learn to forget. But how could I separate the people from the town? The town was made unattractive to young people looking for opportunities. Mainly it was the white people who treated the coloreds like they were still second class, and worked us like slaves. The coloreds didn't embrace education, because their focus was on commerce, making farming a business. We all knew farming could never be a lucrative money-maker as long as the white man didn't pay fair wages. I was glad Robert would be raised in an environment where the most powerful woman in the community was colored and she owned a bank.

As soon as we had put our things away, and Robert was in the bed, Simon said, "I will be going out again tomorrow."

I didn't get upset like I had time and time

again. I had some things I wanted to do too. "I figured you'd have to go. Let me iron your laundry."

"Do you have to do it tonight?"

"I guess I can do it before you leave in the morning."

"I'm surprised at your reaction to me leaving."

"What do you mean?"

"You seem to want me to leave."

"I guess I'm getting used to you leaving. Anything can get old."

"You sure you are all right?"

"Yes, I'm fine."

"You don't have another man walking around here, do you?"

"I can't believe you said that to me."

"I can tell things are different. You are not worried about the sheriff in Jefferson, are you?"

"No, I am just growing up. I realize you have to leave and there is no sense in making a big deal about it. You are going to leave anyhow."

"I sort of liked it when you begged me to stay." He chuckled.

"It didn't do any good."

Simon decided to change the subject, "I can't believe we just left a funeral. Willie was living and smiling like a Cheshire cat at the club. The man appeared proud of his wife and his life."

"I know. Who would have thought he'd be dead."

"We were having a good time until the shots rang out in our ears."

"I can't believe Ms. Pearl has to deal with the loss of another lover."

"I think Pearl moves on pretty quickly. She appears to be a lady with her own plans in life. It is a shame two men have lost their lives."

"Yes, especially Willie, who wanted only to love her."

At that moment, the girl from the club flashed up in my memory.

"By the way, Simon, who was the woman who visited our table at the club?"

"She is just someone I met awhile ago."

"Where?"

"It don't matter. I'm married to you."

"I want to know."

"She ain't nobody, Carrie," he said.

"Well, you are somebody to her," I replied, waiting for a reaction.

"I knew her before we were married."

"But, I thought I was your only girlfriend."

"You were. She is just someone I met at the club one night when we were on a break."

"We are married."

"We were not married. I wouldn't do that to you. She and I had a conversation and that is the end of it," he answered, glancing in every direction but mine.

He didn't appear believable. When he talked about her, he intentionally didn't look me in the face, and the darkness in his eyes led me to think he was hiding something. Simon was one of the most sincere people I knew. He kept promises, and was mature beyond his twenty years. This was the first time I felt he was not telling me the truth, and it bothered me even if she meant nothing to him.

Simon reached over to touch me. "She just wants what you have."

"Why, though?"

"I danced with her one time in the club. I told her my name and I told her about you. She still tried to catch my attention. I don't want her, just like I don't want Nadine. I waited for you. You are the woman I married."

All of a sudden, the fence I had around me fell down. I could feel the sincerity again. I believed what he said. However, the story about one dance I didn't feel certain about.

I soon realized it was my last night with

151

Simon before he was off again. And this time he said he'd be gone a month. They were doing the last of the fall training. Afterward, he would be home for the entire months of January and February. Now that Rube Foster had already established the National Colored League, and Simon played on the associated team on the East Coast, he was headed south to try out for the newly formed Colored Southern League and he had a good chance of playing for the Birmingham Black Barons. If all failed, Simon would continue playing on one of Virginia's independent teams. Simon would not rest until he played next to the greats like Pop Lloyd, Rube Foster or Virginia's own Pete Hill.

"Carrie, this is our last night together for a while. Let's enjoy each other."

"I know." It was the moment my emotions began to kick in. I couldn't wait to be with him. "But, I have one more question . . ."

Simon put his hand over my lips, "No more questions. You are my wife — only you."

He led me to the bedroom. Before I could undress, he lifted me onto the bed, passionately kissing me. He assisted me in peeling off my clothes, first my blouse and then my skirt. He kissed me on the neck and then my back, so passionate I became breathless, and vulnerable to his touch. He used his tongue to titillate my skin, sending chills all the way down to my spine. I kissed his neck, too, and rubbed his hairy chest. His breathing was rapid. I could hear every breath he took. He was anxious, and so was I. After he was fully naked and so was I, I wrapped my legs around his athletic hard body, and inhaled as he entered me in full force. I forgot about everything, and concentrated on enjoying making love to my husband.

CHAPTER 14

I woke up to the aroma of food cooking in the kitchen. Before I could get dressed fully, Simon came into the bedroom with Robert in his arms. He coaxed me back into the unmade bed, and placed a plate of food in front of me. I smiled. He had prepared bacon, eggs and toast. It was the first time I'd been served in bed. I ate as slowly as I could, knowing afterward Simon would be packing his things for a long trip down South.

All morning I expected a knock on my door. However, this time Nadine didn't show up and I found myself smiling from the relief. I had been practicing for over a week on a way to tell her to stay home and find a man of her own. I was tired of her interruptions and passes toward my husband. My plan was to get rid of her for good. Late in the afternoon, as I watched Simon neatly fold his clothes and place them in the duffle bag, a knot came in my throat, as I struggled to find the words to tell him about me going away to school.

"I want to talk to you about something," I struggled to say.

"Please don't start with me about that woman. I told you she is nobody to me," he immediately assured me.

"That was not what I wanted to talk to you about," I said, wondering why he was always on the defensive lately.

He turned toward me, but a frown greeted me. "What is it, then?"

"Nothing," I mumbled. His reaction had silenced me.

When his face finally relaxed, he said, "Come on; tell me what is bothering you."

"It can wait. We'll talk when you get back," I said, escaping from the conversation.

He gazed at me hard. "This time I hate to leave. I've never been gone this long. Will you be all right?"

"I'll be fine. The Halls are downstairs. They are like family. Robert really loves them, and they treat us like family. We will be all right."

"I will be back home as soon as I can," he said, throwing the last pair of pants in the bag.

"You have to be careful going way down south," I said, remembering Bobby, Mrs. Ferguson and most of all the other white people in Jefferson County. "They ain't too keen on socializing or getting along with colored people."

"It's a bunch of us going. We know the way white folk treat coloreds. They are always searching for a reason to hang us or lock us up. We're gonna stick together. When we do stop, it will be at other colored's houses. They will feed us and give us a place to sleep. Besides, I ain't no fool. I can handle myself."

While he was assuring himself, I got up, went into the kitchen and packed up the leftover chicken that had been in the icebox. I put it in a brown paper sack along with several slices of white bread. I put a cloth napkin in the bag also. I knew there would be no place for them to eat along the road. Colored folk couldn't eat at white folks' places. The papers said two colored boys had been dragged and killed in North Carolina. They had been beaten and dragged behind a car until they were not recognizable. The only way they could be identified was by the clothes they were wearing. Simon was not a fearful kind of man, yet I couldn't believe it was safe to

156

travel anywhere alone. I was glad there would be four of them.

"You be careful," I said to him.

He forced a smile, "Now don't worry. I'll be all right." He patted his shirt pocket. "We got papers with us. We got identification. We will be on the main roads all the way. It is two cars of cats trying to get with the Barons. It is four of us, and three in the Chevy behind us."

Deep down I didn't want him to make the team down south. Mrs. Miller, my grade school teacher, said colored people in the South were treated worse than a dog. She told us to try to move north if we could and get away from the Jim Crow laws. She said the South didn't like coloreds and the men who wore the white sheets were as "dumb as a nail." She said they killed just because they could and would get away with it. I couldn't stand the thought of things being any worse than they already were for colored people. We had our own businesses, restaurants and schools; we really didn't need white people. There were a few complaints about the quality of the colored places, but at least we had our own.

Simon handed Robert to me. He kissed me tenderly on the lips and gave me a "month hug" as he called it.

"I love you!" I said.

When he went out the door, Robert and I watched him get into the car and drive through the trees down the street and out of sight.

"It's just you and me, baby," I whispered to Robert.

He pursed his lips to cry, but ended up smiling instead.

I got back in the bed and held Robert close to me. He closed his little eyes and we both went off to sleep.

When the moon had crept out into the dark sky and the stars appeared close enough to touch, we woke up. Robert was a good child. He was nothing like his father. Or was his father like that before the world got to him? I didn't know. Robert was so precious. When I finally opened my eyes in the dark, he was awake beside me, contently playing with his toes. I turned on the lamp. I got up and finished putting together Robert's clothes for my trip to Petersburg, Virginia. I felt bad for deliberately not sharing my information. I didn't think Simon would take too kindly to me leaving Robert for the week. As I laid out my clothes for my trip to Petersburg, tears welled up in my eyes. I didn't know how I could leave Robert either.

Simon had not been gone but two days before Nadine knocked on the door. I opened the door with my arms full. I was about to take Robert's things downstairs to the Halls.

She peeked in my door. "You here by yourself?" she asked, looking around as if she expected Simon to jump out and surprise her.

"Yes," I answered, opening the door wide enough for her to enter.

She sat down in the paisley-colored chair across from the davenport. "My ole man said he saw you on the train," she said, crossing her legs and looking away from me as if I made her sick.

I stared at her before I said a word. My palms were clammy and my nerves were rattled. Nadine had that effect on me. Her annoying and flirty ways bothered me.

"Why were you messing with my man?" she boldly asked.

I cleared my throat and took a deep breath before answering her. "Nadine, I only spoke to him. I don't mess around. I have a husband."

"When I seen him, he come talking about how good you looked," she said as she cut her eyes my way.

"He can say whatever, Nadine. I don't

have any feelings about your husband. All I did was speak to him. He is my neighbor, right?"

"Why did he make it seem like ya'll had something going on then?" she asked, leaning in, her eyes wide open and fully engaged as if I irritated her.

"He was trying to make you jealous, I guess. Maybe he wants you back. Don't you want him back?"

She threw her head back. "He wants me at home all the damn time. I'm too young to be tied down. I ain't that type of girl."

"I understand you, but I have a husband. I don't need yours too."

"Simon ain't around," she snapped.

"But, he is my husband." I put my hand on my hips. "Nadine, listen, I'll say it again. I don't want your husband. I have one of my own."

"You act like Simon is so special. He ain't nobody."

"Nadine, please leave," I said, walking toward the door.

She did not budge.

"Tell me, Carrie, why did he mention you to me?"

I walked back toward her. "I don't know and don't care," I said. "Is there a reason you don't believe me?" I asked. "Why would

I lie? I love my husband."

She smacked her lips. "Sound like you are too good for Simon then."

"Why did you say that?" I asked, watching her body language. She had something on her mind.

"Never mind," she mumbled.

"I'm a woman just like you, Nadine. I know you think I am not telling the truth."

"I can see you are telling me the truth. I don't know why my husband tried to make me jealous."

"I wouldn't do that to you," I said, knowing she would stab me in the back as soon as I turned around.

"Too bad you over here by yourself."

"I don't mind. Simon is doing something he really wants to do."

"Are you sure about that? He is always gone," she said, looking at me, her eyes shifting like there was a reason for doubt.

"Yes, I am."

She shook her head. "Simon probably out there with one of his women."

"You don't know him!" I shouted.

"I've lived across the street from him for over a year. He is no saint either," she said and stood up to leave.

"Sit down, Nadine. What do you know?"

She sat right back down. "Well, I probably

shouldn't tell you this, but since you are so
naïve, maybe I should school you on your
athlete husband." I could see she was upset.
"No, I'd better leave now."

"Nadine, do you have a thing for my
husband?"

"He's all right."

"All right?" I repeated.

"Simon is a handsome man. He used to
be checking me out before he got married
to you."

"Are you married, Nadine?"

"Yes and no."

"So you were interested in my Simon?"

"He is all right."

"He is my husband and not a single man.
Besides, you came over here accusing me of
coveting your husband, while all the time
you want my husband."

"I could have had him before you got
here."

"What makes you think that?"

"I used to see him watching me, winking
his eye when I walked by. He even whistled
a couple of times."

"Nadine, he is my husband. We are together. I do not want your husband and I
would appreciate it if you would act like a
lady, and leave me and my husband alone."

"My husband told me about you. It is the

reason I came over here. I don't want Simon. He used to watch after me. Before you came, he would talk to me. Now he acts all strange."

"He is married and so are you."

"That man ain't my husband. He was just living with me. I don't want to be tied down to no boring man who is never home," she responded, twirling the ends of her curls.

"Nadine, I am so glad you decided to visit me; now I feel I know you. You are a miserable person. You used what your so-called husband said to you in order to pay me a visit. All of it was because you have a thing for my husband. Leave him alone! He is married to me. He don't want you. Find someone you can have for yourself!"

"If I wanted him, I would have him," she quickly shot back. "Do you think I want a man who is gone for weeks at a time? He is good-looking and all that, but he is a roamer. He probably has women all over town and a few down in the country, too. You know any man who is away from home as much as Simon has another woman somewhere. The colored baseball players are famous for having more than one girl, a country girl. So, the truth is you are just like me, lonely. Your man is gone and so is mine. We are stuck at home with the children while they have a life of their own. I don't want Simon. He is too busy in the street. All men are damn liars anyway."

I added, "And don't forget, Nadine, he is also married."

"Before I go, let me just say it. If you ever need someone to go to the club with or hang out with, I'm right across the street. I get tired of men fooling around. We got feelings too. Damn it." She got up and headed to the door.

CHAPTER 15

Gray smoke billowed from under the train's wheels, as it screeched and came to a halt. Adam Murphy stood waiting right beside me. He showed up when I crossed the street in front of the rooming house where he stayed. "I'm going with you to Petersburg," he boldly stated. Petersburg was right next to Richmond. I wanted to say no, but instead I said, "It is nice to have some company with me. I've been a bit nervous thinking about taking this trip alone. I don't know what to expect."

"I thought you could use a friend on the first day," he said. I peered over at his wide smile and grinned.

My hands had been trembling all morning. When I took Robert down the stairs to the Halls, I tripped and grabbed the balusterade just before I started to tumble. It was a miracle I'd maintained my posture with Robert on my hip. He grinned, thinking the shaking was fun. Mrs. Hall had been up early, making sure everything was in place for Robert. She had been sipping on black coffee since four a.m. When she opened the door and saw us, her blue eyes danced with joy. Robert reached for her as soon as he recognized her standing in the door. We walked into her family room. It was a clean place, though somewhat boring. The furniture was simple, a paisley davenport and the typical high-back chair. She didn't have a lot of anything in the rooms. Actually, it was a bit mundane. The furniture was simple. Unlike the walls of colored folk, her walls had pictures of fruit baskets. Even I had a picture of Jesus Christ on my kitchen wall. Everybody I knew had one. On her mantle hung an oil painting of her and Mr. Hall. They were in their thirties, maybe forties, both of them with smiles across their faces showing all of their teeth. They looked as happy in 1900 as they did now.

"I've been waiting for you."

"Yes, ma'am," I said. "I feel guilty leaving Robert here while I'm gone. You know this will be the first time since he has been born that I was not with him at night. It seems sort of wrong."

"Sit down," she said as she handed me a cup of coffee I never asked for.

"You are a child yourself, and you have a life. Robert will never remember you being gone. He is still young. By the time he is old enough to remember, you will be finished with your education. Don't feel guilty about progress."

I sipped the black coffee. It was strong and bitter. I wanted sugar and cream. However, I never asked. Listening to her speak about life surprised me, since white people always had it so easy.

"Can I ask you a question?"

"Sure," she said, rocking Robert back and forth. He snuggled close to her chest, with dreamy eyes, wanting to go back to sleep.

"Why do you know so much about guilt and taking chances?"

She chuckled. "In case you haven't noticed, I live with a colored man. We have been together for over thirty years. I met him when I was a young girl. I knew it was forbidden to fall in love with a colored man. However, I believed in progress. I felt all people were created to be happy. Why should I live my life being miserable because nobody understands my life? It is up to us to change the world."

"Mrs. Hall, my life has always been complicated. I have a baby. I'm too young to be a mother, and I don't have anything to offer my child. My husband is away chasing his dreams, and I daydream about a better life for me and Robert. Simon is a good man, though. He wants to take care of us, but I see more. He wants me home and pregnant, and my momma will be angry because I left Robert with you. I feel bad about what I am doing."

She shook her head. "Listen to me; you're young. You have a right to be happy too. Don't feel bad about taking care of you. Simon is off taking care of his self. Is it wrong to love yourself? Back in 1913, women marched down the streets of Washington, D.C., for women's rights. I went up there and walked right past the White House. It was the Women's Suffrage Movement. Colored women from Howard Normal School marched right beside us. They were in a sorority for colored girls. They took a stand for you. Most of them were in school to be teachers too. There is nothing wrong with progress." Then she patted Robert on the back. "You see, Robert is already asleep on my shoulder. He'll be fine, and we will take good care of him."

I took the sleeping Robert out of her arms. I kissed him and he opened his eyes and smiled. I put him back on her shoulder and he fell right back to sleep.

"Thank you for what you are doing for me."

"It is for your family. You will be happy when you feel better about where you are going in your life. What you are doing is the beginning of something good and new."

For a moment, she reminded me of Mrs. Gaines, a white woman I had found refuge with while working in a job I despised. Working as a white woman's maid bothered me, and is why I wanted to teach. Education seemed to be the only way a colored person could gain an ounce of dignity. Even yet, the lifestyles of most colored folk were not any better than those who worked as servants. The excitement of knowing things gave one a sense of freedom.

I didn't believe white people could be good until I met Mrs. Hall. Her courage in marrying a colored man, had inspired me to do the thing not necessarily popular, but what was the best for me. The only other person I knew who had a relationship with someone of another race was Miss Topsie. She loved white men, but mainly for the money. I can remember the way Mr. Ferguson stared at her when he came into the Feed and Seed store, and she was there purchasing her rosewater perfume. She'd smile and he would tip his hat. Momma would tell me, "Come on, chile, white men are out of order."

I'd respond, "What do you mean?"

And she would say, "Just don't go around no white men when you are alone." I knew exactly what she meant. None of them would be seen with Miss Topsie in public, yet at night when the field animals were sleeping and everybody else was supposed to be asleep, she had a visitor.

"Mrs. Hall, I'd better go now. I'll see you in a few days. By the way, Robert loves mashed potatoes." She softened her eyes, stared at me and smiled.

When I walked out of the door, tears welled up in my eyes. I tried to bat them away, yet they just leaked down my cheeks. I struggled to keep from looking back. I walked down the road toward Adams Street, past the nightclub and crossed over to Broad Street. In my hands were all the things I thought I'd need at the Normal School, a suitcase filled with three dresses, a pair of shoes, underwear and a cloak to stay warm.

In a few weeks, the landscape would change and snow would be on the ground. And, to imagine neither Simon nor I would be home with our child. Both of us harboring a compulsion to make something exciting and worthwhile happen in our lives, everything self-serving.

Adam Murphy surprised me by showing up. He was all dressed up, wearing a dark-gray Sunday suit with a black bow tie. He was almost dressed like an undertaker. He appeared handsome and strikingly manly for someone in school.

"I thought I'd ride down to Petersburg with you."

"But, you don't have to do that."

"I know, but your husband is gone away and you'd be traveling alone. A woman don't have no business making her first trip without a man."

"Adam, I went down there before alone. It is too close to Richmond to worry."

"I know, but today is different."

"How is that?"

"Well, you are leaving home for the first time and you are not coming right back."

"I'm coming back in a week or so," I said, teasing him, and admiring his gentlemanly ways. "I'm glad you decided to come with me. Now I don't feel so alone."

He smiled. "This is the beginning of something good. You know how many people are scared to change?"

"What do you mean by scared?" I asked him as we waited for the conductor to let us board the train.

"Colored people want to do good too. Colored men want good-paying jobs. My uncle works for the government. He is a janitor, but he gets a pay check every week. Some colored men can't do anything but farm. They sell vegetables for a living. It is a hard job, slaving out in the heat, the sun hovering above their heads, beads of sweat rolling down their cheeks. The sun kills."

All of a sudden, I was sad. "I know my papa died from being in the sun way too long."

"Colored men can use their minds too. We have used our backs for too long. I want to be a doctor, or maybe a preacher. Teaching is an honorable job. Everybody wants to do better, but some of us will never get the opportunity. They are afraid of change, and the unknown."

"You are right."

"This is your chance, Carrie," Adam said as if he'd known me for a long time and knew I had always desired to teach school.

"All aboard!" the conductor yelled.

All of the colored people made their way to the last car on the train. Adam and I got on. I panned around looking for Nadine's husband, and was extremely happy when I didn't see him anywhere. The man was creepy. His stares were more than I wanted to handle.

Adam lifted my bags onto the train and then sat down beside me. I couldn't believe he was going with me to Petersburg, just to be friendly. I didn't have men friends and was ashamed I had not encouraged Adam to stay in Richmond. Besides, he was not my man.

We talked about family, children and school the entire ride to Petersburg. One lady made a comment and we both laughed. She said, "You two are the cutest couple."

We didn't tell her the truth. Both of us replied with a simple "thank you."

As we exited the train, we heard someone from a distance calling, "Carrie!"

I turned in the direction of the sound and there stood Nadine's husband waving and grinning like a Cheshire cat. Adam picked up my luggage and began to coax me toward the school.

"Carrie, wait a minute!" Nadine's husband yelled, walking toward me.

I stopped and waited as he approached us.

"What are you doing back in Petersburg?" he asked, even before I could say hello.

"I'm here for school." All the time he was staring at Adam as if he was someone to

173

reckon with. Adam peered at him as well, so serious, I thought something might happen.

"We've got to get going. I have to be somewhere by noon."

"How's your husband?" Nadine's husband asked in a suspicious tone.

"He is doing well, real well. He may end up in the big league one day," I answered.

"I'm sure he will," he mumbled, and cut cold eyes in my direction.

As we walked away, I could feel him still peering at us, but neither of us turned to take a look.

Adam and I walked side by side toward the boarding house I would be staying in. He didn't say anything about Nadine's old man, and neither did I. The fall breeze was just brisk enough to shake the leaves on the trees. It felt good on my skin. I felt free. Adam appeared a bit rattled, but the breeze appeared to relax his face. I was not sure if it was the man at the train station or the mention of my husband, Simon, that made him shiver.

In a platonic way, he grabbed my hand. I didn't pull away. I let him fill in temporarily for my husband who was off chasing balls on the baseball field. Adam escorted me to the house and sat in the sitting room until I had unpacked my clothes. I shared a room with two other college students, women also inspired to educate colored children.

Adam stood as straight as a soldier, his brown face smiling at me as we waited for the evening train to come around the curve. I expected him to be tired or anguished after walking side by side with me around the small country town, familiarizing me with the life at a secondary education school. Along the way, we met two well-dressed girls who were also enrolling in school. Both of them smiled at us, and we introduced ourselves. Surprisingly, they were from a small town too, and being at the Normal School was also their first time away from home.

The evening train came swiftly and right on time. As we waited for the colored porters to assist the passengers with their luggage, Adam said, "I've enjoyed this day with you. When you come home this week-end, please stop by. I'll accompany you on the train home."

"I'm married, Adam."

"All girls need to be cared for."

"All right, I will."

He stood in front of me, grinning. When he put his arms around me, I felt strange. I gazed through the crowd hoping Nadine's old man was not lurking somewhere. He was not anywhere to be seen. The embrace was innocent, and for some reason, it felt right.

"Take care, Carrie, and study hard!" Adam sputtered out just as the train door closed.

"I will!" I yelled, waving back at him.

It was lonely walking back to the Normal School, yet I knew it was the beginning of something grand.

CHAPTER 16

The school was just like I'd imagined. Mainly young girls like me desiring to get into a classroom and teach colored children how to read, write and count. A lot of people from Jefferson never attended school or had quit as soon as they started because they had to work in the tobacco field. Signing a deed was sometimes left up to the white landowner who didn't care at all about them. Many times they were overcharged and even sometimes tricked into giving up their earnings.

Things were going to change when it came to my community. I knew education would be how I'd free myself and my friends. I couldn't help thinking about the letter I'd received from Hester. She said, "This is what you always wanted to do. Do your best."

On the way home on the train, I smiled to myself, knowing a week of studies had been completed and I'd earned my stay at the boarding house. I had with me a leather book and a writing pad.

The weather was changing rapidly. It was chilly and the wind still. It smelled of moisture, and I wondered if snow was ahead. I walked straight over to Adam Murphy's house. It was something I'd looked forward to all week.

Adam was waiting. "I didn't know if you'd be on the early or late train, but I've been waiting for you."

I threw my arms around his shoulders. "School is wonderful, Adam. I've met a lot of friends and new people," I told him, elated about the experience.

"I know you can't wait to see your baby and husband."

"My baby is waiting for me, but my husband is still with the team."

"You will have a lot to catch up on when you get home. Do you have any bags I need to carry for you?"

"I left everything back in Petersburg. There was not a need to drag them home with me, when I'll be heading right back in a few days."

He got on the trolley with me. I filled him in on the week's activities.

As we got off the trolley, Adam tightened

up the scarf around his neck. He and I walked down Broad Street past the government buildings toward Jackson Heights. When we came to the bar Ms. Pearl sang in, I convinced Adam to go in with me to find her. She was there, sitting in the empty room with her pianist. She immediately recognized me when I walked through the door.

"Hey, girl, why are you here so early? The show doesn't start until sundown." Her pianist got up and walked over to the bar.

"Who is the fellow with you?" she asked.

"Oh, this is Adam, a friend from school."

She grinned. She was without the heavy makeup, and even appeared younger than when she was all made up. "Your husband was in here last night. He said he was headed back on the road again," she said between sips of something that looked like water.

"It must have been someone else, Ms. Pearl. Simon is still out of town," I said as I sat down in the empty seat beside the piano.

"Oh no, it was him all right," she said and pointed toward the bar. "He sat right there and talked to me for a good half hour."

"Good," I commented, puzzled, "he must be home early."

"Probably so," she said. "He was in here

last Saturday night too. I asked him about you. Did he tell you?"

"No, ma'am, he must have forgotten," I lied.

"What made you stop in here today?"

"I wanted to see how you were doing since Mr. Willie passed."

"I'm doing good. Willie was a good man, just too jealous," she said, shaking her head. "I miss him, though. That man loved me."

"He appeared to be a nice man too."

Adam stood beside my chair quietly absorbing our conversation.

"Like I said, he was good, but a little too jealous. I'm an entertainer. I have to keep my customers coming back fo' mo'."

"Have they found the killer yet?"

She raised her voice. "There ain't no damn killer. He brought it on his self. You just can't jump in nobody's face for no reason. Willie had a temper, and that's what killed him."

Even though she had a smile on her face, I could feel a little frustration in her voice. She didn't like my last comment, so I quickly excused myself. "I'm glad you are doing good, Ms. Pearl. I ought to get on home now."

"It was good you stopped by. How's your baby?"

"He is getting bigger."

"Keep him away from the mess. If he is anything like his daddy, he's got some slick in him."

"No, ma'am, he is just like Simon," I quickly interjected.

"He's got some shit in him, too," she said.

All the time, Adam Murphy was quiet, listening to everything and without a doubt absorbing every word like a sponge. His eyes sparkled with curiosity, either from meeting a star or from listening to our conversation, one which had my face turning pink.

She peered over at Adam and smiled. "Glad you ain't like some of these women sitting around waiting for a man to come home."

"Adam is just a friend, Ms. Pearl."

"Everybody needs a good friend, chile. Don't feel bad for having a friend. I'll bet Simon has several women friends. Don't be no damn fool for no man."

"Yes, ma'am," I mumbled.

"You don't have to say ma'am to me. Just call me Pearl. If you need someone to talk to, come see me."

As we were turning to leave, the white man from the club appeared.

"Who are these people, Pearl?"

"Just a couple of friends," she answered,

as we turned to walk away.

He seemed inquisitively nice. I studied Ms. Pearl before I walked away. I made note of her mannerisms when the white man entered. Her composure was the same. He didn't have the same effect on her, that Momma said Willie did. Ms. Pearl wasn't scared of him.

Adam asked me as we turned onto Adams Street toward my house, "Are you going to be all right? Ms. Pearl said your husband was home."

"I don't know, Adam. Seems like things are changing."

A concerned frown swept across his face, and his eyes appeared worried; all the time his brown eyes were squinted like he was thinking intensely.

I also had something brewing in my thoughts. On three different occasions women had orchestrated doubt concerning my husband's devotion to me. No one had ever said anything about him to me. He was the good guy, the one who opened his heart to me and to Robert. Simon loved me and I loved him. What was said bothered me, even made me sad. Why would they say those things?

When we made it to the gate of my house, I couldn't let Adam come in. I said to him softly, "Adam, I think it is best I deal with everybody before I introduce you to them."

"I will leave, if you think you will be all right."

"I am fine. My neighbors, the Halls, are like family to me."

Adam hugged me in front of the apartment gate.

"I'll be going."

As he walked away, I yelled to him, "I'll stop to see you on my way back to school!"

He turned and waved, but he didn't smile.

I watched him until he disappeared through the oak trees and was out of sight, headed back toward the college. Then I knocked on the front door.

Mrs. Hall came to the door. Robert was in her arms, clinging to her like he was glued to her.

"Come on in, Carrie," she said.

I reached for Robert and he jumped into my arms. I couldn't resist smiling.

"You miss me?" I asked him.

He just smiled from ear to ear.

"Mrs. Hall, was Robert a good little boy?"

"He was real good. He is a happy child and so easy to care for."

"I'll take him out of your hands for a few days."

She laughed. "Tell me all about school."

"It is everything you said it would be. I love my classes and the students are real nice. My living arrangements are okay. I share a room with two other girls."

"Is that all right with you?" Mrs. Hall asked.

"It is probably a blessing. I am learning how to study and work from them. We cook the meals and clean for the owners. So far, we have a plan."

"Good. I knew it would work out."

Then I asked, "Has Simon been home, Mrs. Hall?"

"Nobody has been here, but us. I thought he was going to stay away for a few weeks."

"That is what he said."

"You sound like you doubt it."

"It's just people say they saw him. I'm wondering if he is really out of town."

"Now don't read too much into what people say."

"I won't, but it all sounded so real, Mrs. Hall."

"What did they say?"

I told her about Nadine coming over and about Ms. Pearl saying he had been at the nightclub. When I told her about Ms. Pearl, she sucked her teeth. "What's wrong, Mrs. Hall?"

She tucked her head. "Nothing, I tell you;

184

nothing at all, Carrie. Now don't spend too much time worrying about it. Just talk to Simon when he comes home."

When the words flowed out of her mouth, they seemed forced. It felt like an empty statement without conviction. When she changed the subject, I knew something was up.

She handed me Robert's things. I picked up the bag and started toward the door. I looked back at her, and she turned her head.

When I got home, everything was the same way I'd left it. I looked in the ice box and everything was still the same. I went into the bedroom and the bed was made the way I'd left it. How could Simon be in town? Where was he laying his head?

I unpacked my small bag, fed Robert and washed his clothes by hand on the washboard. I hung up his things on the clothesline in the bedroom. Then I said my prayers, and Robert and I curled up together and went off to sleep.

The next day around noon, I put the sweater Momma had knitted on Robert, and he gazed at me, waiting for me to pick him up. I threw on my coat and with Robert on my hip, we marched across the street to see Nadine. I couldn't wait for Simon to decide to come home. I wanted to know what was going on.

Nadine answered the door after one knock.

"Come on in," she said as she opened the door wide.

I stepped inside. Her two children were sitting at the kitchen table eating biscuits.

"Y'all hurry and finish and go on into the front room. I'm going to make me and Carrie a cup of coffee."

Her little girl got up from the table. She cleaned the crumbs away and put the dish cloth in the sink. "Can I hold him?" she asked, and pulled Robert from my arms. He smiled at the sight of other children.

"To what do I owe this visit?" Nadine asked, smiling.

"I wanted to talk to you about something."

"I knew you would come calling sooner or later. Have a seat, now that I have my kitchen back."

The table had been cleaned and both children were in the front room playing with Robert on the floor.

We pulled out a seat at the wooden table. Nadine poured both of us a cup of coffee. It was the afternoon and I usually drank coffee only in the mornings. After adding sugar and cream, I sipped. "Nadine, I'm a young wife. I probably don't have the

186

experience you do with men. Simon is the only man I've ever loved."

"Carrie, I know you didn't come over here to go through your entire history with me, stuff like where you come from and your momma's first name I think you have a more serious reason."

I cleared my throat. "Well, you said something about Simon that has me worried."

"What is so confusing? Was it what I said or how I said it?"

I took a sip of the coffee since all of a sudden my throat was dry. I needed help getting out the words and making sense as I spoke. I inhaled and attempted to get my thoughts aligned so I could find out what I needed to know.

"I'm waiting," Nadine said, twirling her long tresses as she always did. It was a habit you'd expect of a young girl.

"Nadine, you made mention of Simon and a girl the last time we talked. Could you explain what you meant to me."

"I'm not sure you have it right. I never said Simon had a girl. I just suggested that you wise up, girl."

"What did you mean?"

"Carrie, are you completely naïve? Your husband has been living in Richmond for some time now. He lived across the road there before you came here. Now, do you really think you are his only girl?"

"Yes, Nadine, I do; at least I did."

Nadine shook her head. She reached over and tapped me on the hand. She raised her voice. "You are young, but don't be a damn fool!"

"I'm not a fool," I responded. "I am in school now. I will be teaching students real soon. I'm not a fool."

"I didn't mean you couldn't read or write. You need to take care of yourself. I know Simon will continue to be Simon."

"Nadine, I don't understand what is wrong with Simon. Is he seeing someone else?"

"He is a man, isn't he? He ain't no different than most men. You just got here about six months ago. Do you really think he was sitting in a corner waiting for you?"

"No, but he is a good man. He has never hurt me. He is probably the best man I've ever seen."

"Even the best men can go astray. Everybody needs a little loving. Simon is like my ole man. When he sees something that looks tasteful, he will pursue it. That is how we first got together."

I listened with ears as big as an elephant; the word *together* bothered me.

"I was minding my own business at the bar where your Ms. Pearl works, when Simon came over to me. He approached me with a very wide smile, one that covered his entire face. Simon grabbed my hand, and told me he needed company, wanted someone to talk to; so I sat down."

"I thought you were happy with your ole man. Why would you be in a night spot without him?"

"You asked me a question, and now you don't want me to answer."

"Nadine, I just want the truth."

"Okay, he asked me to have a drink with 'em, and I did. A woman came by and rolled a cold eye at me. I just knew she was his woman, but he denied it, said I had seen something different. And yes, I was with Jessie, but he was off on another one of his trips." She peered over at me. "You know a woman needs company too."

"He is my husband, Nadine!"

"I didn't know about you. I didn't think he had anybody. I saw one woman come out of his place the entire year he lived alone, before you came."

"What woman? What did she look like?"

"Listen to me, Carrie. You appear to be a naïve, country girl type."

"I am not naïve."

"You need to know that whatever he does in the dark will come to light. Just wait and see."

"Have you seen him in the last week?"

"No, I have not."

I couldn't help feeling Nadine had been naïve too. The seriousness in her eyes indicated she had been fooled once. I knew she wouldn't be fooled the second time around.

"I ain't seen nobody across the street. You ain't been there neither."

"I thought maybe Simon had been home. I'm in school."

"So I take it, the little boy taking your books is in school with you. You are a bold girl, Carrie."

"Nadine, that man is a friend. Simon is whom I love."

"Most women don't realize men are like us. They need attention and someone to tell their secrets to. Maybe you are more like Simon than you think."

"What do you mean by that?"

"I think sooner or later, you are going to get tired of being the good little girl at home waiting for her husband to make it big in the Colored League. You will start to live yo' own life. That's why I'm sort of glad my ole man left. He wanted me to live in seclusion and wait for him to return home, after he'd been chasing coat tails all day long. A friend told me he is always at the station waiting for some pretty girl he can charm."

I shook my head. "Why do you have to turn things around?"

"Did I hit a nerve, Carrie?"

"You just seem so detached from what I was trying to ask you."

Nadine cleared her throat, "Simon is a man. If he had a woman in the house before you came, it wouldn't change nothing. All I'm sayin' is, you should not be no fool. How hard is that to understand? You a grown woman with a child; now act like it."

I walked out feeling more confused than when I came.

CHAPTER 17

I tossed and turned all night waiting for Simon to show up. I kept watching for the door knob to turn, anticipating him walking through the front door. Robert could sense my tension. He whimpered one time before rolling back over, closing his eyes and falling back to sleep. I silently waited as the stars came out and danced across the sky, and the moon ascended in the heavens shining bright through my bedroom window, and although I must have fallen to sleep, I still remembered when the sun came out and lightened up the sky. About two a.m., I woke up, and went into the kitchen. I searched the cupboard for the wine Simon had brought home, given to him by an old lady from our hometown. Elderberry wine was not my favorite, but anything to help me sleep. It was the nastiest-tasting drink I'd ever tasted, yet when I finished the last half of the glass, my eyes had begun to hang heavy and off to sleep I went.

I waited to hear from my husband all weekend long, but there were no signs of him. I didn't receive a letter either. So, I packed my clothes and got ready to return to school. I forced myself to only think about making my grades and doing my little job cleaning and washing, which allowed me to stay in the rooming house for free. Simon was not around, but everything in the house was paid for. I tried to dismiss my thoughts about my husband, and focus on something else, but him missing from home, yet seen around by others, had my nerves rattled and my mind perplexed.

The weeks flew by.

Robert seemed to be very comfortable with the Halls. Simon was his father, but Robert would never know him if he was always off chasing dreams. Now I was doing the same thing.

One morning, I got Robert dressed for his trip downstairs, dressing him in the baby-blue sleeper Momma had knitted. He was so cute, almost like the doll baby Momma made me as a child. I didn't want to go back to school without telling Simon about my new life as a student. I never was a good liar, and always felt bad when I stayed after school with Simon and let him kiss me and rub me, but never on my private parts. It was disgraceful for a girl to lie, but for Simon, I'd do anything. Now, I wasn't sure how he would handle it, or how he would feel about it all, but I had to come clean. I didn't want any secrets between us, although from the mouths of the neighborhood, he was holding them from me.

When we got down to Mrs. Hall's apartment, she was cooking for her husband. He was smiling from ear to ear and staring at her like a dog in heat. As much as they stuck out in the neighborhood, they had a different relationship than many couples. It was as if the forbidden fruit was more tasty. He loved her and whatever she desired, he honored. On the stove were beans and cornbread. And no matter how it tasted, he would say it was the best in town. Everybody knew white women couldn't cook. Mrs. Hall was nice, though, down to the core. She forced me to look at color from a new perspective. Before meeting Mrs. Hall and her starry blue eyes, I felt any white person around was a monster, except for Mrs. Gaines, whom I often wondered about.

"You ready to get back to school so soon?"

"Yes, ma'am. The holiday will be coming quickly and I will be home for a few weeks."

"Well, we will take good care of our little

boy. Having Robert has been a joy for us. He keeps us young and he is such a smart child. Do you know he is trying to walk?"

"No, ma'am, he didn't do anything for me."

"Did you put him down on the floor?"

"No, I was so glad to be home with Robert, I let him wrap his tiny legs around my waist and I toted him around the house the entire time. You think he will walk for me now?"

"You've got to be patient with him. He will do it when he thinks no one is looking."

"He's a typical man. They do more when no one is looking."

It was that moment I thought about my husband. He had not been around for weeks, yet everybody had seen him. It had me thinking.

Before I left, we tried to get Robert to walk, but all he did was sit on the floor, then get on his knees and crawl toward Mr. Hall. When Mr. Hall reached down to pick him up, a smile spread across his little face. They were good to my boy. Just seeing the smile on his face eased the fears I had about leaving him behind.

"It is about time for you to get going."

"I guess I will get to the station."

"Wipe that look off your face. You know, you will be home in no time."

"I feel so guilty."

"Now, don't start that again. Everybody want to do better for themselves. You've got a little boy to raise."

As always, Robert and Mrs. Hall stood in the doorway and watched me until I was out of sight. I walked through the neighborhood past the corner store and then two blocks over right past the nightclub where Ms. Pearl worked. I wanted to look in. However, it was too early for the all-night-ramblers.

I didn't stop at Adam Murphy's as I had in the past. I didn't want to lead him on. He liked me and I had a certain feeling about him. With Simon's absence, I could envision our relationship growing to a level that was not good for me.

The train was virtually empty in the colored section. There were only a few people riding on Monday morning. The short trip to Petersburg was soothing. I had learned how to close my eyes and take a nap, like the others on board.

"Petersburg!" the conductor yelled.

I had with me a bag of clean clothes and I had made some biscuits to keep in my room in case I got hungry. I had lost a few pounds since I had been going to school. At night, after washing the dishes and cleaning the kitchen in the boarding house, I would be hungry. A buttered biscuit would have been a perfect supplement for the late-night studying.

I looked for Jessie, Nadine's man, when I stepped off the train. He was there, but staring at the distant sun. He waved at me and walked my way. I stood there waiting to hear from him as if he meant something to me.

"Good morning! Where is your friend?"

"He goes to another school."

"Oh, so is he your friend?" He chuckled.

"No, we are fellow students and the time you saw him, he was helping me orient myself to the school."

"Wonder if Simon knows about him."

"I hope they will be friends."

"Do Simon know the other fellow is escorting you around Petersburg?"

"We are only friends. There is nothing for him to know."

With each comment, I was getting more nervous. Jessie had me rattled.

"I don't have anything to be ashamed of. I have not done anything wrong."

"Yet," he interjected.

"I am a married woman, Jessie."

"I know that."

197

"Look, I really need to go."

"I'm here if you need a real man."

I gazed at him, and glanced away. He was a bold man without any reservations. When he looked at me, his eyes took a trip from my face to my feet. It was an inappropriate stare, much like the one from Mr. Camm. I didn't like it, even though he wore his porter's uniform well.

After I got unpacked and settled at the boarding house, the lady of the house knocked on my door.

"Carrie, can I come in?"

"Yes, ma'am."

She entered the room for the first time since I'd moved in. She glanced around the room, and then complimented me. "You keep your room so neat. Is that your room-mates' stuff over there?"

"Yes, ma'am."

I didn't know why she was visiting me, and I wondered what I had done. She sat down at the desk in the room.

"You had a visitor while you were gone."

I didn't say anything. I couldn't figure out why I would have a visitor at the boarding house; only a few people knew I was in Petersburg.

"Who was it?"

"It was a fellow."

198

Adam didn't tell me he was coming to town, I thought.

"Did he leave a message?"

"No, but he is back. He is downstairs waiting to see you."

"Okay."

"Now this time I will let you receive this visitor, but you must tell him you only can receive visitors on Saturday and Sunday evenings. The rest of the time is for studying. Y'all colored girls have got to be the best to teach. We don't need the interruptions of our studies started by any young men."

"I am sorry."

"Don't be," she replied, standing. "Just make sure it is clear to your visitor. You can see him for a few minutes. You can even go out with him, as long as you are back before eight o'clock this evening."

"I will. Thank you."

She walked over to me, and tapped my shoulder. "You are on your way up, and distractions are everywhere."

"Yes, ma'am," I said and walked out behind her. We went downstairs to the parlor. When she opened the door, my eyes nearly popped out of my head.

"Hi, Carrie!" he said, and stood up. The dimness of the room revealed a silhouette that had been missing for weeks.

"Hi!" I said, gathering myself from the shock, and peering at him from the door.

Simon reached out for me, but I was still at the door. I inhaled deeply. I wasn't sure what I wanted to do. I placed one foot before the other, my feet paralyzed and heavy like they were in quicksand. Did I want to hug my husband, or did I want to slap him instead? Simon gazed at me with concern in his eyes, his eyes steady and his arms reaching.

"Come here," he demanded.

I walked over toward him as the landlady watched.

He put his arms around me and held me tight. I shared his embrace, thinking what a strange surprise.

"Who is this man, Carrie?" my landlady asked, brushing her hands along the side of her A-line skirt.

"This is Simon, my husband."

"Hello." She walked over to us and shook Simon's hand.

Simon smiled.

"I didn't know you were married, child."

"Yes, ma'am."

"He still can't be here for over twenty minutes. If I let him stay, the rest of the girls will want to do the same. Now, you

200

can go outside and talk. Just remember, eight o'clock is your curfew."

"Let's take a drive, Carrie. I will have you back before eight."

I followed him out the door and down the stairs to his car. All the time my mind was wondering how he had managed to come to Petersburg. I couldn't wait to hear. He had come here secretly, and maybe secretly he'd been in Richmond the entire time.

Once he had driven across the railroad tracks, he pulled the car to the side of the road. "How you like it down here?"

I immediately began to explain, "Simon, I was going to tell you. I am going to school now. I want to teach children."

He let his hand roll off the steering wheel and turned toward me. "Why didn't you let me know?"

"I didn't think you would like it. You think women ought to be home raising children."

"You are a mother now. Somebody's got to take care of Robert."

"I know it. I want a career like you do," I said. "Robert is in good hands."

"Where is he?"

"He is at home with Mrs. Hall."

He was quiet. The only sound was the motor of the car which was still running. The sun was descending and there were no other cars around. Finally, he said, "All you had to do was talk to me."

"Simon, it seems we both have secrets."

"Why do you feel that way?"

"You've been in Richmond, but you didn't come home."

He cleared his throat. "I came back to Richmond one time. I didn't come home because it is so hard to leave you and Robert. I didn't know you were not even there."

"We are your family. Why is it that everyone knew you were in town but me?"

"I hate to hurt you. Every time I leave, you have tears in your eyes. It tears me apart."

"I should have talked to you about school and you should have come home. We were both wrong."

"Yep. Is Robert okay with Mrs. Hall?"

"He loves her. I come home on the weekends. When did you last see him?"

His facial expression changed. His eyes narrowed and grew concerned. "I am going to see him tonight when I get home. You should have told me what was going on."

"I thought you were down South training."

"I am back now. I'm going to be around for a while."

I smiled at the thought of him being

home. I just wasn't sure how he would handle me being away all week.

"Do you want me to quit school?"

"No, I want to know what you are doing. I can help with Robert."

This was the Simon I had fallen in love with. He cared for the world.

Nightfall was coming fast and we had another hour before I had to be back at the house. He pulled me close to him. My heart raced at the warmth between us. His lips were soft and wet. He laid me down on the front seat of the car, cracked the window and we let the cool breeze dance across our skin. He kissed me, and I suddenly started to melt. He lifted my dress and pulled down my bloomers. He unbuckled his pants and without hesitation, he put his thickness inside my moist legs. I lost my concentration with the first thrust, and my breath was taken away. When we were done, we pulled everything back together again, and he started the Model T. We drove back out of the brush and across the railroad tracks to the boarding house. When we got there, he handed me a few dollars for food.

"I'll see you when you come home this weekend."

"How did you know I was here?"

"Nadine told me; she knew exactly where

to find you."

"Where did you see her?"

"She was at the club."

"We have so much to talk about. I need to know where you are. Nadine shouldn't see you more than me."

"Nadine don't mean nothing to me. She is just a girl across the way."

"I'm young, but not a fool."

"I know you are smart, Carrie. Tell your friend Adam you are married."

I was stunned when he brought up Adam. Had he been following me all along? Or was he going by what Nadine had told him? Whatever the case, Adam was no threat to him.

"He is just a friend."

"Carrie, I am the only man you need."

"He is a friend."

"I hope that is all," he said.

CHAPTER 18

Pearl Brown Jailed. Ms. Pearl had been arrested for Willie's death. People said it was a murder for hire as I read from the letter I received from Momma. The entire town was still in an uproar over Mr. Camm and now Willie. *They were trying hard to link Ms. Pearl to both of the murders,* her letter said. She had a connection all right; both men were obsessed with her for whatever reason. Ms. Pearl loved the attention of men, but a murderer? I doubted that.

I remembered both incidences vividly. Mr. Camm was found on a path between his house and the juke joint. He was drunk too. People said he was beaten, but his death came from a gunshot wound. People said Pearl was afraid of the accusations because Willie wanted him dead. Aunt Ginny had asked me, "Did you kill the bastard?" Her serious green eyes nearly scared me to confess.

"No, ma'am," I told her, shaking, and ashamed she thought it was me.

"Well, if you did, I wouldn't blame ya. He was a dirty son of a bitch."

Her eyes were like those of a cat and her stare more frightening than most. It was as if she didn't believe me. But I knew she hated him too. She was a no-nonsense type of woman, and I felt she would do whatever needed doing to protect her family.

"I wanted to kill him my damn self, but somebody got to him fo' I could get to him. You see, don't nobody mess with my family. I ain't gonna stand for it. That man hurt you and somebody needed to teach him a lesson," she told me the same day he was found frozen with his face kissing the ground. When she spoke about him, there was a certain degree of coldness in her voice. She turned red as a beet when she was upset, and those green eyes of hers became dark and mysterious like those of a cat.

Momma was also someone who wanted Mr. Camm gone, even if she never admitted it. There was no way a woman with her commitment to Christ and the church could continue living a lie with Mr. Camm. From the first day he knocked on our door, shortly after Papa had allowed the sun to claim him, and died, I sensed Mr. Camm would be trouble. He was a well-dressed man with mysterious dark eyes that followed women no matter where they were. He did it the first time I answered the door. The way he sized me up was an inappropriate gaze for a stranger.

I caught my brother Carl polishing the rifle one day when Momma was away working for Mrs. Ferguson. He never said a word about Mr. Camm, yet I knew he disliked the man as much as anybody. I didn't understand his sudden obsession with rifles. When Papa taught him how to shoot, he would say, "I don't like rifles. They can get a colored man around here in a lot of trouble."

Talk is Mr. Camm had more women than Mr. Johnny, who was known to mesmerize and take women on a journey few men could claim. He had three of the church ladies at one time. None of them fought or said anything to one another. Two of them had children by him. He served on the usher board and even tried to be a deacon, but the church folks told him to let two of the women go and stick with one. He refused, and said, "If I can take care of 'em, they ought to be mine."

The preacher told him, "Well, you won't

be no deacon in my church." Momma used to tell the story often. I knew Mr. Johnny, and he never did anything to young girls. He respected most women, except he had three of his own.

Mr. Camm had a slew of folks wanting to hurt him. Willie was a good fellow; he was so preoccupied with Ms. Pearl that he did some things I am sure he regretted.

Everybody said, "Pearl don't deserve Willie; he is too good for her. She needs somebody like her, in the streets. Let the street people prey on each other." The church folks always had a comment for anyone who did not sing holy praises all day. Ms. Pearl being arrested was something her fans did not want to hear, especially those of us in Jackson Heights. When Momma wrote me, I was a little upset since I had visited her earlier that fall. She had been honest and warned me about Simon. I knew she did not kill Willie because the white man in the club did it. I was there. Her time in jail would be quick because even if she had murdered her husband, coloreds killing coloreds were not a big interest to the law. The white man who shot Willie was probably the one who would get Pearl out. White people had been getting away with lynchings and killings for as long as I remember.

There were parts of Richmond I didn't dare to walk through because colored folk always had limitations, and that would never change.

After reading Momma's letter, I started to think about Adam. I put away any thoughts of Mr. Camm and his murder. I didn't want to be a part of nobody's investigation. I had not seen Adam since he had visited me a few days after Simon left. I was glad to see him, although Simon had warned me to leave him alone. He came dressed in a dark wool jacket and trousers, and was wearing a hat. He wasn't the sharpest-dressing man, yet there was something distinguished about him.

I was in the room I shared with two other girls — one of them married like me, and the other single and looking for a man with his own business. Most colored men who were in business did carpentry work or worked with metal. They transferred their blacksmith businesses into metal making when people started purchasing automobiles. The white folks depended on them to make the wrought-iron fences and even the beds they slept in. Mariam wanted a metal man for a husband.

"They make a good living," she said.

"Why are they better than farmers or even

baseball players?" I asked her the day before Adam showed up. We had just finished going over some grammar our teacher felt was suitable for teachers. She expected us to articulate every word and write good letters, since writing was the center of our education.

Mariam was a real dark girl, and along with her beauty, her smile lit up a room. She was smart, too. Her parents had sent her to Virginia to study. They felt Petersburg was a quieter place than Washington to get her studies. She liked it, too, but her focus was to go home with a teaching diploma and a husband with a business.

"Carrie, your husband is never going to make the kind of money you want. He will be forever chasing his dreams."

"Why would you say something like that?" I asked her, folding up the laundry.

She grinned and turned her head to the side like a bashful little girl. "Because the Colored League is never going to be recognized like the white players. My momma told me that some of the best players are colored and no one ever recognizes them. I just tell it like it is."

"Things are changing. There are leagues being formed all over the East and out West too. They can't keep them from trying."

"I suppose you are right, but it is hard to see a future with a baseball player. Now your friend Adam is going to be somebody."

"He is still a colored man. No matter what he chooses to do, he cannot change the color of his skin. Besides, I am married."

"He ain't coming down here for nothing."

"We are friends and friends only."

"He is mannerable and sort of cute."

"Simon is polite and handsome," I teased.

"He is. I saw him the night he came to visit. We were looking out the window when you got in the car. He could be considered beautiful, but he ain't no businessman."

We giggled. I loved the two girls I shared my room with. We all had the same desire, and we never competed for anything. I would often speak of Hester to them. I missed her so much, especially since I never seemed to get a chance to go to Washington, D.C. for a visit.

Mariam and I had just finished the washing when Adam came. This time, he had a small package in his arm.

"I bought you something," he said.

Before even saying thank you, I commented, "We are not supposed to have visitors on weeknights."

"I know, but it has been over a month

since I've seen you," he said, taking off his hat.

"Well, let me grab my coat and we can walk somewhere." I took the package and went back to my room to get my coat. I tore open the brown paper wrapping before going downstairs. In it was a book written by my favorite poet, Paul Lawrence Dunbar. It was a special moment, and I longed to spend the evening hours thumbing through words which sang songs in my ears.

The temperature had begun to shift. Fall was here in earnest. The days were short and the nights long. The leaves had all turned and the ground was covered in a tapestry of colors. I loved the fall and especially the sweet elderberries, which were ripe for picking. Momma had always made elderberry jam in the fall. That season was almost over, though. Adam and I began our stroll at the boarding house and ended it on the school yard. We walked hand in hand. Adam had filled in when Simon was away. The long talks on the train around the subject of school made me more eager to study. Now, I was faced with telling him I could not see him anymore. How do you tell your friend he cannot come by? How do you isolate your friends from your family? All of those thoughts buzzed in my head as we walked across the school yard and found a seat on the school house steps.

"Did you open your present?" he asked.

"It was one of the best gifts I've ever received."

"I know how much you like poetry. You said Dunbar was your favorite." Paul Lawrence Dunbar was the only poet I knew. Mrs. Ferguson made sure we read his work in school and now at the Normal School, he was one of the writers we study. I liked his love poems and often thought of myself when I read his work.

"I knew you would like the book; I knew it," Adam said, smiling.

The moon was high now and shining down on us. It was a clear night, chilly without a breeze.

"Where will you stay tonight, Adam? The train has already left."

"I have someplace to lay my head for the night. My mother's sister lives here."

Adam was a good friend, and maybe, if I was not married, he would be more. He had a particular seriousness about his self. He was smart; he would speak about the stars and the way they were shaped in the sky. He pointed out the Little Dipper, the Big Dipper and the Lion. He told me the stars were always smiling. He even had a certain

213

liking for the Greek philosopher, Aristotle.

"I value our friendship, Adam," I said, thinking about the role he had played in my boring life.

"Me, too," he said before I could finish.

"I don't think we should continue seeing each other, though."

"Did I do something to offend you?" he asked, concerned.

"No, it is not right for a married woman to spend so much time with a single man."

"Did your husband tell you to stop talking to me?"

"Well, it does bother him."

"I know. He told me to leave you alone. I tried to tell him you were my friend, and he wouldn't listen."

"So, he came to see you, too."

"Yes, he did, but I am a man. I make my own decisions." His expression was washed with emotions. I wasn't sure if it was anger or loss. Did he feel he was losing me as a friend or was he angry because Simon had been so controlling? "If he continues to be absent, I will certainly step up. You are too young to be left alone."

"I told him we were only friends. I can't understand why he came to see you."

"Carrie, a man can sense when he is losing. He knows I mean you well. I told him that much."

"But we have not done anything," I said, hurt because Simon had taken matters into his own hands, and had not trusted me.

"We are friends and that is the beginning of all good relationships."

"I don't want any trouble. I don't want Simon to think the worst of me."

"Maybe it is his own guilt he is worried about." His comment made me uneasy. I inhaled deeply to keep from commenting about what I'd been told about my husband. Nadine, Pearl, and even Mrs. Hall knew something.

"Whatever the reason, I can't see you anymore."

"I appreciate your honesty," he said, grabbing my hand.

It felt strange holding his hand after saying I didn't want to see him. His hands were warm and thick, and his eyes more serious than ever before. There was something special about him. He reminded me of Simon when we first met. He was caring and patient.

"I won't try to convince you of anything. Carrie, if you or your baby need anything, you know where to find me. I don't like your decision. However, I understand."

We stood up, turned up our collars, covering our necks from the night air, and headed back to the boarding house. He held my hand as usual. When we got to the front door, our eyes met with a compelling magnetism. He pulled me close and kissed me hard on the lips. It was something he had never done before. I was without words.

"Write me. I need to know you are studying hard," he said.

I was still shocked from the kiss. It was unyielding and pleasant at the same time. It felt good, even though I should have been upset.

"I will," I answered him and watched him walk down the street swiftly toward the darkness, toward a neighborhood where most of the coloreds lived.

CHAPTER 19

Simon had been home the entire fall break. He even had cultivated a relationship with Robert, where when Simon left the room, Robert squirmed and waved his little arms until he came back and picked him up. Things appeared strange with Simon at home. He had not been home for more than two weeks in the last four months.

Mrs. Hall had been upset ever since he'd come back. While I was away, Simon dropped Robert off late at night and picked him up the next day. She didn't like how he did things, said it was confusing for Robert who was on a schedule.

I welcomed his presence. And for the first time in many months, my husband was home with me and my son. We were a family again. Simon had been getting up early in the morning, carrying out the chores of the house. He fed the chickens and gathered the eggs. Mr. Hall had been doing it for us.

They were like family to me. A white lady in the early 1920s posing as a colored girl's mother, with a colored husband. They were true mavericks in the neighborhood. It was strange, but everyone, especially me, needed a family away from home.

"Carrie, I need you to talk to Simon about Robert," Mrs. Hall said the first morning I was back from school.

"What is wrong?" I asked her, reading the seriousness in her eyes.

"Simon's been keeping Robert up past his bedtime, and he is waking up cranky. Children ought to be in bed by eight p.m. You must speak to him."

"Why didn't you tell him, Mrs. Hall?"

"I tried to talk to him, but I know he didn't listen to me because he did the same thing again night before last."

Simon being home was obviously causing a few problems. What wasn't making sense was him dropping Robert off late at night, several hours beyond his bedtime. Any changes in his schedule would certainly make him cranky and interrupt Mrs. Hall's gardening and puzzling. She spent her mornings in the yard, even when the leaves were falling off the trees, cutting back the chokeberries so her hydrangeas could bloom in the spring. Afterward, she would do word puzzles, something I knew nothing about. I had never seen a puzzle until I came to Richmond, and Mrs. Hall was working one. She purchased the *New York World* paper once a week from the newsstand, basically for the local news of her hometown and the word puzzles.

"I'm sorry for this. We will not do it again." I said it knowing Simon would be the person who had to do the most changing. Now I was curious why was he leaving so late at night. Where did he spend his evenings? Along with the changing temperatures, Simon was also preoccupied with something or someone.

The first snow was falling, the flurries spinning in the air and topping the ground like a white blanket. The wind was calm. I was home, waiting for the holiday season to pass. I had arrived just before Thanksgiving. I couldn't help thinking about Adam. Was he all right? Did he get an A in all his subjects? I had all As in spite of the newness of being away from home, and having a baby. I would say raising a baby, but Mrs. Hall had taken on that task without any complaints. I was proud of myself. It wouldn't be long before I would be teaching my own class of students.

Adam listened to Simon. I had not seen

him for a month. Simon had interrupted a good friendship. Simon was always good to me even though I had started to wonder if he was telling me the truth. Pushing past the memories of the stories of him coming in and out of town had not been easy. His visit to Adam was something I didn't know if I could forgive him for. I was his wife, not his possession. Now, he had Mrs. Hall upset. The hours he was keeping had me questioning his whereabouts.

Simon was home every night before the sun went down. He'd come home with a plant in his hand on Tuesday, said he had been downtown talking to one of Rube Foster's men about a permanent job with an East Coast Negro League.

I waited until Simon had finished eating. The green curtain in the kitchen window was swaying from a breeze coming through the window I'd opened to let out the scent of the fried cabbage I'd cooked for dinner.

"Simon, Mrs. Hall had a talk with me today. She doesn't like it when you drop Robert off past his bedtime."

"What is she talking about?" he asked with frown lines across his forehead.

"She is trying to keep him on a schedule. It is easier for everybody that way."

"She is too attached to Robert. She don't

have no children herself and she act like he is hers."

"No, the Halls are like family. While you were gone, they sort of became parents for the both of us."

"I appreciate them, but Mrs. Hall is going to ruin the boy. She is going to have him thinking he is a white boy."

"Simon, she is a good lady who happen to love our child. Please don't put crazy thoughts in your mind. The Halls are family."

"Uh-huh," he mumbled.

His response concerned me. "The point is, you can't take Robert to them real late at night."

"I wouldn't have to take him there at all if you were home with him."

"I am home almost every weekend while you are somewhere! Who knows where?" I raised my voice.

He got up from the kitchen table. "What is this really about? Is this about Robert or me?"

"Both!" I yelled.

He stood in front of me reading the scowl on my face. "What is going on?"

"Simon, you are leaving late at night. You are dropping the baby off too late for the Halls. I have a question. Why are you going out so late at night? You are a married man."

"Now wait a minute! It is not what you think."

"What is it?"

"I got me a little job."

"A job? I thought you were out playing baseball."

"I am. But, when I need a little money, I work at the club."

"So, I guess that is why everybody sees you around town, but me."

"You can't believe everything you hear. Have I ever let you down?"

"No, never. I just want you to stop taking Robert to the Halls so late."

The words were missing. I couldn't think of what to say. All I could see was him standing before me, towering over me and words seeping out of his lips. My responses had not been on point. Most of it was words, lacking focus.

He tried to touch me and I pulled back, and pushed his hand away.

"Calm down. I will take Robert before eight, if that will make you happy."

"Yes, please," I said, shaking my head.

"Carrie, believe me, everything I do is for us," he pleaded.

"I want to believe you. I really do," I replied, still perplexed by the conversation.

He put his arm around me. Although I was still filled with mixed emotions, I let the conversation end without tackling the job at the club. I exhaled a breath of frustration and walked away into the sitting room.

I sat in the high-back chair, stoic, with Simon standing in the door frame, Robert crawling curiously on the floor. I stared out the window at Nadine's house and the church tower. The snow flurries had stopped and the road was clear. Everything seemed to be in order except for my mind. This was the first argument I'd ever had with my husband and it felt worse than a whipping.

"You all right?" Simon asked, peering at me from across the room.

"I'll be okay," I answered and reached down to pick up Robert who was at my feet.

"Just know everything I do is for us."

I nodded my head yes.

The next night, Simon was out real late again. When he returned from the club in the early morning hours, he had a fistful of greenbacks. He was a gatekeeper or bouncer, as they called the men who kept order. He enjoyed it, and was big enough to put a little fear in any hooligans causing a ruckus.

It was going to be a long two months being at home. Each day I started my morning out the same. First, I cooked breakfast, and then got Robert dressed. Later, after the chickens were fed and the house cleaned, I'd sew clothes for Robert. He was a chunky child and was growing out of his clothes faster than I could make them. I needed to be home. I patched Simon's socks and sewed on buttons. I made up for the time I had been gone.

Simon rose early. He would tend to the chickens and care for Robert while I was cooking and attending to the household chores. It was as mundane as it had been in Jefferson. It was a lonely quest keeping house. All day I took care of everybody, and Simon and Robert thanked me with wide smiles.

"Are you cooking for Thanksgiving or are we eating with the Halls?" Simon asked as I finished washing the last dish and turned it over to drain. Although it was my first Thanksgiving in Richmond, cooking a big feast had never crossed my mind.

"Momma wants us to come to Jefferson," I quickly responded. "We can invite the Halls to come home with us. They don't have anybody. Mr. Hall said all of his family is gone from around here."

". . . a white lady staying at May Lou's?"

"Yes. We are all God's children, right?"

"You know what I mean. The people of

Jefferson don't take too kindly to white women and colored men. Too many colored men have been killed because they settled with a white woman. I don't need any trouble."

"They will be at Momma's. They are not going to church with us. Besides, we are only going to stay one night."

"Next year, we are going to have dinner here."

"I can't cook all those pies and cakes like Momma."

"You can learn. Maybe you should ask her a few questions while we are there."

"Questions?"

"Yes, ask her how to make some of her recipes. She will tell you."

Me being at home had him in some sort of daze. His imaginings of me cooking and cleaning and having a dinner feast did not sit right with me. I didn't mind cooking for my family, but Simon seemed to be a bit overboard, almost excited when he talked about me preparing delicious dishes for him, especially the kind Momma made. The next thing he would want to do is invite the entire Colored League to sample my cooking.

CHAPTER 20

The Halls had a hard time making the decision to go with us to Jefferson County. Mrs. Hall was fine with the idea, but Mr. Hall had some deep reservations.

"I don't want no trouble down there. Folks can't understand us."

"Everybody knows it, George," she said. It was the first time I'd ever heard his name. Most of the time, she referred to him as Mr. Hall.

Then he added between puffs of his pipe, "We would have had a much better life had we gone to Canada like we planned. People don't understand us. I'm sort of glad we don't have children. I know they would be mistreated."

"George, why are you bringing up all of that? The child just wants to know if we will be going with them to her momma's for Thanksgiving dinner."

"Don't say I didn't warn you. People

down South are different. Hell, the people right here in Richmond barely speak to us."

"We are used to it. After thirty-five years, nothing surprises me," she said, smiling and shaking her head at the same time. "Carrie, we would love to go."

She cut her eyes over at Mr. Hall. He grunted, but didn't dare say anything else.

I was so excited to hear her answer. After being around them for the past eight months, I had forgotten about the color difference. They treated us like family and we did the same for them. Mrs. Hall would often bring up homemade cookies. Her oatmeal cookies were mighty fine, but no one could make them like Momma. It was the thought, anyhow, which mattered. The only two white ladies I'd known before Mrs. Hall were Mrs. Ferguson and Mrs. Gaines and neither of them had a knack for cooking. I supposed it was the reason they hired someone else to do the job.

Robert sat between me and Simon. Mr. and Mrs. Hall sat in back. It was a good morning, the temperature hovering around 68. It was warm for a fall day, especially since two days before the snow flurries had been dusting the rooftops and blanketing the ground. There was a breeze stirring, and the trees were leaning to the left. Everyone was ready to go when Nadine walked up to the car.

"Y'all going somewhere?" Nobody saw her come out of the house. She showed up from nowhere.

Nobody was quick to answer her. I sucked my teeth and Simon inhaled.

"Where y'all going?" she asked again.

"We will be back tomorrow," Simon answered, without telling her everything.

"Okay! Well, I'll watch everything until y'all come back home."

"We won't be gone that long."

"Okay," she answered in a sad tone. "I'll see y'all when y'all come back."

When Simon pulled off, Nadine was still standing in the street. It was the first time I'd seen her since I'd come back home from school.

The Halls had never traveled to Jefferson County. The only place they frequented was Petersburg on occasion, and Washington, D.C., they said. A place like Jefferson surely was not a place they even imagined visiting.

When we came to the point where the paved road became dirt, Mrs. Hall sat straight up.

"We really are going to the country. I haven't been in rural areas since I was a child. Upstate New York has plenty of places

228

with dirt roads. I remember as a child taking a long trip by train to Niagara Falls. We traveled through small cities and all I would see was small shanty houses and lots of farmland."

"I grew up in a rural area," chimed in Mr. Hall. "I never liked it. I found the lifestyle boring and too safe for me. That is the reason I joined the service. I had to figure a way out from the South."

"Do you think most people are like us, Mr. Hall?"

"What are you saying?"

"Well, I wanted to leave, too. I didn't like the mundane way of living, especially after my papa died."

"I reckon all of us are searching for something. Living in the country makes it easier for the mind to wander. Every day is the same. Repetition can bring on boredom. And who wants to live a boring life?"

"It's not like you do so much now," Mrs. Hall commented.

"I know. But, if I want to do something like take a walk to the corner market or go to a picture show, it is all very convenient. Folk in the country never see picture shows. Some of them have never been anywhere but from home to church. It is an isolated life."

"Some people enjoy the isolation," Simon said, and then added, "I wouldn't mind living in the country again. Robert would have plenty space to run and play. Carrie could can our food. I'd do the farming."

I cringed at his comment. Amazing how he felt about country living when he was the one who was the first to leave.

"I think it is a place I could visit, but living down here in the brush is something I couldn't do. I suspect I would be bored stiff. I couldn't walk to the market," Mrs. Hall said.

"Most people don't own a car, so they use a horse and buggy," Simon volunteered.

"I'm fine with that. Folks ride them in Richmond," Mrs. Hall said.

Finally Mr. Hall added, "I guess where there is love, I could stay. As long as I am around good people, I possibly could live in the country."

Everybody, including little Robert, broke out in a chuckle. Going home was not hard. I loved it there at times. The star-filled skies and the fresh air was good for anybody. It was the repetition of work that bored most folk. And knowing most of the men would die from heat strokes and exhaustion made me sad.

Route 460 led us straight through the

heart of town. There was a seed and feed store, a post office and a courthouse. Along the James River was a farmer's market where farmers came to trade goods and services. It was also the place where the tobacco farmers hauled their crops after harvest.

We rode past the Fergusons', but I was embarrassed to point out Momma's place of employment. I supposed the Halls knew most of the women were domestic workers. It was mainly why there was so much racial tension. Colored folk did all the things the white farmer felt he was too good to do. It was those memories which inspired me to leave. I knew I would leave even before Mr. Camm walked into our door. I knew I would leave in primary school when Mrs. Miller told us about Washington, D.C., the nation's capital. Her stories thrilled me. When my brother John left for school, I would be leaving right behind him. Simon had his ideas, and so did I, and living in the country was not one of mine. I had my own plans for my future. I thought playing baseball was his goal. I envisioned me home in the country alone with Robert and the four walls, and him traveling the globe, stopping in occasionally while I became a house slave.

Momma was on her way into the house when we pulled up in the yard. In her hands were a bunch of baby turnip greens she'd harvested from her winter garden, and a few onions.

"Mrs. Mae Lou, let me get those," Simon said, hopping out of the car. He opened the door and took the greens out of Momma's arms. She walked over to the car.

"Y'all get on out."

She saw the Halls. "Y'all come on in."

Mrs. Hall got out and followed Momma into the house. Simon and Mr. Hall got the bags out of the trunk, and I picked up Robert.

Inside the house was the aroma of food being prepared. The sweet potatoes were boiling on the wood-burning stove and the mixture of scents had my stomach growling for food. Mrs. Hall quickly found a seat in Papa's high-back chair.

I could sense a bit of discomfort in her. However, she handled it well. Her pale white skin was now pink . . . I suspected it was because she'd never visited the country before. Momma came into the sitting room. "Come on in here, Mrs. Hall. Let's get this dinner started."

Mrs. Hall glanced around the room at Mr. Hall who had taken the luggage into the boys' bedroom, and was sitting comfortably on the davenport with his pipe in his hand.

"Go on, honey. I'll be right here."

"Where can I wash my hands?" Mrs. Hall asked, getting up from the chair.

"There's some warm water on the stove. I put a towel and cake of soap on the bed in the other room. The washbowl is sitting on the vanity." Mrs. Hall appeared lost as she walked toward the bedroom. I got up and followed her down the hallway.

"Mrs. Hall, you need any help?"

"No, I got it. It's been years since I've done this, but I can do it." She chuckled before going into the bedroom.

Momma heard us and commented, "It ain't hard to learn to wash your hands."

"Momma!"

"I'm kidding, Carrie. Folks from the city don't know about our ways. We don't have running water inside. Our water comes from the well."

"You are right," Mrs. Hall said, as she entered the kitchen. "I haven't poured my own water in a long time. I do remember when my daddy put the water pump inside our kitchen. We pumped water straight from the well and we thought it was a miracle. I was a little girl."

We all chuckled while Mr. Hall and Simon

discussed baseball in the sitting room. I had never heard Mr. Hall make so much chatter. We could hear them all the way in the kitchen.

After Mrs. Hall had taken a seat at the table, Momma handed her a paring knife and some Irish potatoes she had been keeping in a sack underneath the house. She said if you kept vegetables in dark, cool places they would last awhile. She canned them, too, except she liked the fresh ones for potato salad.

"I haven't been around this many people for the holiday in a long time," Mrs. Hall said, peeling the potatoes like a professional.

"What on earth do you do for the holidays?" Momma asked.

"George and I usually have dinner alone. I usually bake a chicken and we have pumpkin pie for dessert."

"I'm glad you came down here. My other son is coming home and Ginny will probably come for dinner tomorrow. We like to gather together for the holidays."

Momma was right. I remembered the holidays. We would have the entire church over to eat. Momma was the best cook around and she knew it. She and all the women would gather in the kitchen and everybody had a task. I even helped with the peeling. Preparing a good meal was one of the things she took pride in and it would be so tasty, people would say that she "put her foot in it." One of the things she took pride in was preparing a good meal for her guests. And tonight was not any different.

As Momma bounced Robert vigorously on one knee, I couldn't help wondering how she really felt about a white woman sitting at her kitchen table. Mrs. Ferguson was the only one who'd ever been in Momma's kitchen. Several times I had witnessed her in the same kitchen chair as Mrs. Hall, drinking coffee, once when Mr. Ferguson drove Momma home in his Model T Ford, and again the day Papa died. Neither of the times did Momma smile, yet this time, it was different. On her first visit, Mrs. Ferguson asked me, "When you grow up are you going to cook like your mother?"

Momma didn't say a word. I was only coming through the kitchen on my way to get a glass of water. All the times I had reluctantly walked down the dirt road past the blackberry patch with Momma to cook and clean her house, she had never said so much as a word to me. Most of the time our only communication with her was when she gave a directive like "don't forget to dust under the table; I got company coming."

235

Momma's response was always, "Yes, ma'am." I would cringe. Mrs. Ferguson never even peered my way without batting her lashes and frowning as if she were in pain.

"I don't think so, ma'am," I answered her.

"Why not?" she asked, in an insisting tone, and added, "It's a good living."

"No, ma'am, not to me."

"Most colored children love to cook," Mrs. Ferguson continued as if she were an authority on colored folks.

Momma didn't mumble a sound; I cringed, bit my bottom lip and inhaled as deeply as I could.

"Chile, go on into the bedroom and do your homework," Momma said in a serious tone. She could sense my rage.

"I'm finished," I responded.

She cut her eyes at me, and fear washed over me. "Go on back there and read over your work again," she instructed.

I tucked my head and went into my room, but not before cutting my eyes across the table in Mrs. Ferguson's direction, and hoping she would go home. She was a lady I truly despised. Her manner of looking down her nose at me and Momma shattered my nerves — the gall of her.

Mrs. Hall was different. She knew about

the challenges of the Negro. Falling in love with Mr. Hall in a time when colored men were being murdered for even looking at a white woman in the face was a controversial decision. Mr. Hall was blessed to be still living. Even in the 1920s, colored men were not supposed to be bothered with white women. They were just trouble, some of the ole-timers would shout. After Momma's warm welcome, Mrs. Hall was no longer flushed. Her jowls were relaxed, and her shoulders rounded. She was comfortable.

I had gotten a can of pickles from the cupboard and Momma was making a dressing of oil and egg whites. Potato salad was something we usually made in the summer, However, Momma loved to serve it at Thanksgiving.

We had all finished cooking and prepping for the next day when someone knocked on the door.

"Who is it?" Momma asked, wiping her hands on the kitchen towel.

"Oh, Lord, we don't need Bobby stopping by here tonight," she mumbled as she walked to the front door. She gazed out the window. "I don't recognize this vehicle," she said. "Lord have mercy."

The knocks became intense. She cleared her throat. "Who's out there?"

There was not an answer. Simon went into Momma's room and came back with the shotgun. Mrs. Hall was red as a beet, and Mr. Hall was sweating like a hog.

No one said a word. The silence had me worried.

Momma opened the door and there stood my brother John, smiling from ear to ear.

"Lord, John, you gonna fool around and get shot."

He came in. "I know y'all colored folks was scared to death." His eyes popped out of his head when he noticed Mrs. Hall standing beside her husband.

CHAPTER 21

Ms. Pearl had been locked up for more than two weeks. Bobby had her locked up at the station and wasn't letting anyone in to see her. It was to be expected. For years, Bobby's law was just like his daddy's. His daddy was a cold, red-necked man who, at every chance he got, put shackles on colored men. Now Bobby had stooped to a new low and was harassing colored women.

"Bobby is beside his self," Ginny commented between the dressing and turkey on her fork.

"If there is no evidence against Ms. Pearl, then why is she still in jail?" John asked.

"She is probably guilty," Momma said, as if she had seen her pull the trigger.

"This place is still the same and so are the people," John said.

Nobody said a word, but I could read the concern on the faces of Mr. and Mrs. Hall.

"What are you saying, boy?" Ginny asked.

239

"Colored folks are the judge and jury. They think Ms. Pearl is guilty because of her lifestyle. Folk around here have adopted some of Bobby's ways. They don't believe in themselves."

"If she hadn't of been so much of a floozy, none of this would have happened."

"Momma, Ms. Pearl didn't pull the trigger. She didn't make no one else pull the trigger. My guess is she is as innocent as the people in this room."

Momma rolled her eyes at him, and sucked her teeth. Ginny cleared her throat and took a sip of water. "Well, she ain't no saint."

"Aunt Ginny, we can't accuse her of something she didn't do."

Mrs. Hall appeared lost and out of tune with the conversation, drifting away at times and then interested and concerned.

"Who is Ms. Pearl?" she finally asked.

"She's a singer at the club in Jackson Heights," Simon answered.

"Why is she in jail down here?"

"She is being held for another man's murder. Bobby is just picking with her, since he can. He claims to have jurisdiction even down here," Simon said.

"Y'all got to get together and do something about it," Mrs. Hall said.

240

"We colored," Ginny said, raising her voice. "What in hell can we do about all this going on? Ain't nobody 'round here gonna listen to coloreds complaining."

"Well, ma'am, something should be done. You can't hold somebody in jail just because you can. You need to have a legitimate reason. Being colored is not a good reason."

Momma sucked her teeth. "We don't need to get involved in Pearl's mess," Momma said. "She is a lowdown, dirty snake."

"Momma, she is not that bad," John said. "She's a product of this racist society."

Mr. Hall shook his head in agreement like he wanted to testify to John's remarks, but he didn't mumble a word.

Carl and Mary listened intently to the conversation, and neither of them said a word. Carl squirmed in his seat and seemed moved by all the words being slung across the table. All the talk about the murder appeared to make him uncomfortable. He was rubbing his hands together and his head was lowered. His wife was quiet as a mouse, fumbling with her wedding band. Finally, he spoke up, "Can we talk about something else? I'm tired of the same thing coming up."

"This is news. It is the only thing the people around here want to talk about,"

John replied.

"Did you know the preacher is planning on building a house down the road from us?" Carl asked.

"That's not news. It is boring in comparison to Ms. Pearl. I've been gone from home for some years now, and the only things of interest to the people around here is what happens when somebody dies. We could talk about voting rights and fair treatment for coloreds, but who would be interested? Camm and Willie being murdered is the biggest story around these parts. The last one was when Miss Topsie got raped by the deacon."

"Now leave Topsie out of this," Momma said.

"It is the truth, Momma," John said, refusing to be quiet.

"Even so, leave Topsie out of this. Pearl and Topsie is nothing alike."

"I was talking about news."

"Well, you know Topsie loved the 'tention of men, too," Ginny said.

"She never did anything out of the way with our husbands. The deacon did her wrong."

I bit my lip. I fought to control my thoughts. Momma had been one of the churchgoing women who had said, Miss

Topsie asked for it when the deacon had his way with her. Miss Topsie packed up and moved from Jefferson after they turned their backs and pretended as if it was all her fault. Now Momma seemed to have a different memory of it all. I knew all the time; it was the deacon who was out of place. And he was a man of the church!

The Halls enjoyed the chat, the expressions on their faces changing with each comment. Finally Ginny said, "Well, we know Bobby is wrong. I guess one of us needs to say som'thing to 'em. That boy done made a lot of colored folk suffer."

Momma cut a cold eye at Ginny. "Ain't nothing we can do!" she said in a sharp tone.

"There is always something we can do," John argued.

"What?" Carl asked.

"I am a lawyer. I can go see the sheriff and have a little talk with him."

"Now, John, leave it alone; you still a colored man, no matter how much education you get," Momma said.

"We all know how the sheriff is. He is going to continue treating us wrong, arresting us whenever he feels like it, if we don't say something," John said with authority. I was proud of his convictions and was enjoying the dialogue thoroughly.

"Pearl is not your family," Momma said.

"I know, but she is a colored woman."

Mrs. Hall sat straight up in her seat. "So would you do something if it was a white woman? All women get mistreated."

Mr. Hall tapped her on the knee to silence her.

"I don't like wrongdoings, especially to coloreds," John shot back.

Being outspoken is how John had always been. As a young boy, he'd gotten in a lot of trouble for his tongue. I remembered when Mrs. Ruth, our Sunday School teacher, slapped him right hard in the lips. She wiped the smile off his face. It was embarrassing, and Papa got him, too, when he found out about it. He took a strap to his behind. He learned a lesson, but he still never hesitated to speak his mind. It is the reason we all rejoiced when he said he was going to be a lawyer. You sort of need a quick and deliberate tongue to argue for people. He had not changed.

"You didn't answer my question," Mrs. Hall reminded John. Mr. Hall bit his lip, and tucked his head.

"I would defend you, Mrs. Hall. I am for righteousness and justice."

Her face relaxed and a grin rolled across it.

Ginny relaxed her face. I had watched her green eyes squint and turn into slits when Mrs. Hall asked the question. Whenever she was perplexed, her eyes were the first to reveal it.

"You need to leave Pearl right where she is," Momma commented, picking up the soiled plates from the table.

"I agree with Momma; leave it alone, John," Carl pleaded.

John cut a serious eye in Carl's direction. Carl noticed and lowered his head. Afterward, John kept gazing at Carl from across the dinner table. It was as if he felt something was going on. I knew John; he had always been rebellious. He had defined his own path long before Papa passed. Even a few comments would spark a curious notion in his mind.

"I hope everyone is enjoying dinner," John said.

"The food is fabulous," Mrs. Hall replied, fidgeting with her napkin.

"As usual, Mae Lou done put her foot in it; this dressing is real good," Ginny said, smacking her lips.

"It is pretty good, if I can say so myself," Momma added.

Simon and I glanced at each other and smiles rolled across our faces.

After dinner was over, all of the women pitched in to help clean the kitchen. Mrs. Hall seemed to fit right in. Ginny was having such a good time; she decided to spend the night. John slept on the davenport, and Ginny shared Momma's bed.

Mr. Hall and John played dominoes until the wick in the lamp burnt down. Afterward, they had a stiff drink and we all retired for the night.

The next morning, shortly after breakfast, I took a ride with John straight to the jail house. I sat in the car while he walked confidently up to the jail house door, his dark suit fitting him like it was made especially for him. He had a serious look on his face.

"Be careful," I whispered, when he opened the car door.

"I'll be all right," he said, adjusting his bow tie, and flattening out his suit jacket.

I silently prayed for him. I didn't know how Bobby would handle a colored man with education. I was sure he'd get nervous, since he had always gotten away with dirt.

John knocked on the door. The sound was intense and strong. I inhaled and held my breath. I grabbed a piece of my hair and twirled it in nervous frustration. I was afraid for my brother. Bobby was a cold, white man. He was known for calling us niggas and fools. His reputation was tarnished. We only tolerated him because he was white. And the community in Jefferson County was fearful of the white man. When the door swung open, my heart felt like it was coming out of my chest.

I cringed when John went inside the jail. I sat still, locked in fear. I wasn't sure about the time he was in there, but it seemed to be forever. Thoughts clouded my vision. I watched the trees swaying and heard the wind whistling. All I could think of was Momma pleading with John to stay away from Bobby. Just as I'd convinced myself to get out of the car and go see about him, John came out the front door. He was not alone. Ms. Pearl was holding on to his arm as if he was her crutch.

We were about to pull out of the jail house yard when the sheriff rushed up to the car, his face flushed red, cold sweat trickling down his cheeks. "Now listen here, Pearl Brown, if I hear of any other person you know dying, at the blink of an eye, I am going to put your black ass back behind bars. You hear me?!"

"Yes, sir," Ms. Pearl answered, nodding.

John glanced up at him, his face unyielding. "We are about to leave now."

"Y'all get gone!" the sheriff demanded.

John drove out of the yard with Bobby still standing, watching with a defeated look.

We took the left turn right back to the house, but instead of turning down the road to Momma's, we took the road by the sycamore tree. "Thank you. I thought I'd be in jail the rest of my life." Ms. Pearl's smile had disappeared and the jovial way she normally flirted with men, was not there any longer. Her face was minus the heavy makeup and her eyes were sad. She appeared innocent for the first time ever.

"You are welcome, ma'am."

"I promise to pay you once I get out of here and am back working."

"Don't worry about the money. I'm happy you are free."

Tears welled up in her eyes. "It is nice to see you, too, Carrie."

"Thank you, Ms. Pearl," I said.

She turned and walked away. We left her standing in her momma, Mrs. Annie May Moore's door.

I couldn't help wondering where the white man was who had killed Willie. *How could he leave her in jail this long?* I was positive Ms. Pearl knew the answer.

CHAPTER 22

We left Jefferson in the evening. John, intrigued by the notion of a murder unsolved, decided to remain in Jefferson a few more weeks to do some investigating of his own.

Momma turned up her nose, and placed her hands on her hips. "You need to get on up the road. Staying here is a waste of time. Ain't nobody going to own up to that killing." With an expressionless face, John did not murmur a word.

Momma shook her head, and sucked her teeth.

As we road back up 460 heading to Richmond, Mrs. Hall said, "I think what your brother did is honorable. I wish people had stood up for us."

I didn't understand what she was saying, so I refused to comment.

"When we were first married in New York, people would walk right up to us. Most

249

would speak to me and ignore George. It was a cold and evil thing. I didn't like how they treated him."

"That's the past," Mr. Hall said and peered out the window at the tobacco fields dormant for the winter.

"When old man Freeman arrested you for no reason, I wish we had a lawyer like John around. He is not afraid."

"What happened?" Simon asked.

"It was a long time ago. Freeman didn't like seeing me with a white woman, so he tried to get rid of me. He told a lie, said I'd stolen money from a stash of greenbacks he kept in the safe."

"What kind of business did you work at?"

"It was a hotel. I was the maintenance man. I made all the repairs, kept things running."

"How did he connect you to a safe? Sounds like something at a picture show."

"Freeman took the money and then had me arrested for stealing it from him. I never touched the man. He warned me, he would get rid of me. I stayed in the slammer for over a year. It wasn't until his wife came forth and told the authorities the truth that I was released. If my wife had not been her friend, I would still be locked up."

"I guess we all could use a good lawyer at times."

"It is not easy for us coloreds. John is a strong brother," Mr. Hall said with conviction.

All of a sudden, I felt important. The Halls had an enormous amount of respect for my brother. Although I was worried about him staying in Jefferson, there was a certain amount of pride I held for him and the way he handled Ms. Pearl's situation.

We made it back to Richmond before nightfall. The Halls enjoyed their visit to the country and all of us returned with packed meals for the next day. Momma had carved turkey and packed dressing. She had wrapped slices of cake for dessert. The brown paper bags were loaded with the leftovers.

It was a quick trip, and all the way back, Simon had inconspicuously rubbed my thighs the entire ride home. As usual, Robert had been asleep. I had forgotten about the people of Richmond when we heard a voice, "Y'all done made it back home?"

Nadine's voice made me cringe. Simon grabbed my hand, and we walked up the stairs and went into the house. Robert was still sleeping. The sun had begun to go down, so we put Robert in his bed, and we

251

followed suit.

It was as if no one mattered. Simon pulled me close and put his tongue in my mouth. Before he went on, I excused myself to the bathroom. I pulled out the sponge I had wrapped in paper under the sink cover. I inserted it way up in my vagina. I knew another child was not for me. I returned bare, my full breasts moving with me and my personal spot exposed. I climbed on top of Simon, who had also undressed, and straddled his hips. The teasing in the car had me heated. I couldn't wait to make love to him. As he cuddled his head on my breast and put my nipple in his mouth, I became loose. I felt like rubber. I couldn't control myself. I moved my hips up and down and back and forth until Simon sang out a moan. Simon went fast to sleep. Afterward, I lay peacefully and peered at the stars from the window, searched for the Big and Little Dipper. The moon was bright, casting a glare through the window. I followed it until my eyes became heavy, and for a moment, Adam Murphy flashed across my thoughts. I closed my eyes and smiled.

It felt normal having Simon home. I looked forward to cooking and cleaning. However, I longed for the days when I would return to Petersburg and finish my education. We fell into a routine. Simon left early in the mornings and returned late evening. I would have dinner prepared; we ate and then talked for hours at a time. Occasionally, Mrs. Hall would watch Robert while we attended a picture show or took an evening stroll. Nadine was always watching, like she had an investment in us. Neither of us gave her any time. Simon ignored her and so did I. It was as if she were a stranger to us. It was well with me since she had been so aggressive with my husband, but for Simon, I could sense uneasiness and a mysterious expression at times when she would try to spark up a conversation.

"How y'all do tonight? It's getting cold out here; the winter coming fast," Nadine said, standing watching us from her porch wrapped in a wool shawl.

I waved as we crossed the street heading toward the club where Pearl used to sing. Simon didn't do anything; however, his eyes spoke for him. He gazed up at her and lifted his eyebrows. It was like speaking.

The club was different without Ms. Pearl. It was plain now. The three members in the band made up the make-believe quartet. They played without a songstress and we listened. Heads were not bobbing, and no one danced. It was so mellow, I became sleepy. The business types preferred the addition of a performer with the band.

"When will Ms. Pearl be back?" I asked the waiter after he set a soda on the table.

He smiled. "You miss her, too? She is supposed to be back before Christmas — maybe next weekend."

Ms. Pearl was the show girl and everybody missed her sultry voice and rich sound. Simon and I vowed to return when she came back.

It was strange having Simon home. The subject of the Negro League was gone and forgotten. Simon didn't mention it. We all were aware of Rube Foster, owner of the Chicago American Giants and his efforts in expanding the Midwestern teams. He was the key organizer and wanted to see Negroes get the recognition and exposure they deserved. He had teamed up with Tom Wilson out of Nashville, Tennessee, who was organizing the Southern League in a big way. Together, they were creating leagues with the hope of playing against the white ball players. I knew all of this had to be on his mind. I thought about teaching every day. Now, we were a young couple surviving in the city. I wondered how long the blissfulness would remain.

Simon left early Monday morning for his job at the club. He said he'd be home late because they had to clean up after the weekend crowd. He was everything to the club: the bouncer, the waiter and even the janitor. I got up as usual, got Robert dressed and started my day. I washed Robert's clothes by hand and hung them on the back-porch clothesline. Since I had been home, Simon had been home almost every night. I left Robert sitting in Mrs. Hall's lap while I walked to the corner store. The owner was glad to see me, as usual. I had not been in there but twice since I'd left for school.

"Your husband comes in here now and shops. Where have you been?" the owner asked as he stood at the counter wearing his red butcher's apron.

"I'm in school." I waited for him to cut the sharp cheese.

"Education can get you places," he commented as he pulled out the hard cheese.

Just when he handed me the hard cheese all wrapped up, I could feel someone standing behind me. The air seemed to be compressed, like someone was breathing down my back. I hesitated before I turned around. When I turned to look over my shoulder, Nadine was standing close to me with her arms folded across her chest.

"You think you're cute, don't you?"

I inhaled before I replied. I felt the warmth around my temples. "What are you talking about, Nadine?" I asked, not really caring what she had to say.

"You know what I'm talking about. You and yo husband holding hands walking down the street. I spoke to y'all the other day and nobody opened their lips."

"Nadine, I waved at you," I said, and walked around her toward the counter to pay. She followed close behind me.

"Y'all act like I ain't your neighbor."

"We have our life to live, Nadine. You are not family, but I always speak."

She pointed her finger at me. "Girl, don't let Simon mess over you. You act like he the only man on this earth."

I turned to face her. "He *is* my husband."

She smacked her lips.

As I walked to the door to exit, she continued to talk. "Wait; I am going to walk back with ya. Let me get some flour."

I wanted to tuck my head and run. However, it would've been considered rude even if she did deserve it. I waited for her to purchase flour and lard.

On the way down the street, Nadine appeared more at ease, less bothered with us not speaking. I loved the cobblestone streets in Richmond and how they made the street seem rich. My path to my house in Jefferson had been a dirt road. It was a peaceful walk, even with Nadine as company. She didn't say much, only small talk about cooking for her children. It wasn't until we were almost at the fence in the front of my yard when she decided to antagonize me one last time. "Carrie, you a good girl. Simon is out in the streets."

"How do you know so much?" I asked her.

"I know men like him. He is the kind with all the charm. You think about him all the time. When you fall for him, he got you."

"What makes you an authority on men?"

"Jessie back, ain't he? I treat 'em like they do me. It is the only way to handle them. Simon got you all wrapped up."

I frowned and said, "Good day."

She sashayed across the street with a bounce in her stride. She had finally gotten what she wanted to say off her chest. I knew Simon had been around. He had left Jefferson over two years ago. It was enough time to figure out how to survive in the city. Besides, traveling around the Eastern Shore had taken him to places he never thought he'd go.

Dinner was prepared and ready to be

eaten when Simon came home. I didn't mention anything about Nadine, yet for some reason, I was glad Jessie was back. Maybe she would mind her own business. I wanted to forget everything she'd said, but could still feel the tension from her words radiating with me, and I couldn't help cogitating on it all.

Chapter 23

My brother John came to visit a week before Christmas. He stood in the doorway brushing the snow off his lapel, and studying me with a serious scowl on his face. He was a handsome guy, average in many respects, and sharp as a knife. He was usually jovial, but for some reason he came, this time, with a frown.

"Can I come in?" he asked, so serious I felt a chill, his chocolate face shining from the sun's glare.

"Come on in." I opened the door wide. He stepped inside with a leather briefcase in his hand.

I had many questions for him, especially since we had left Jefferson County knowing he was on a mission.

"Have a seat," I said.

He didn't go into the sitting room; instead, he pulled out a seat at the kitchen table. I poured him a cup of coffee, and then took a seat at the table across from him. "To what do I owe this visit?"

"I'm on my way to D.C. I thought there were some things we needed to talk about."

I shifted my weight in the chair, took a deep breath and waited.

"You seem a little nervous," he commented.

"Well, I don't know what to expect. You haven't smiled yet. You worry me when you are this serious. What is going on?"

"I just dropped Ms. Pearl off at the club. I gave her a ride back from Jefferson."

"I didn't know you and Ms. Pearl was so close."

"We are not. She asked me to be her lawyer and handle her business. But Pearl is not the reason I am here. I need to talk to you."

"Now you've really got me worried," I said, sipping on the bitter coffee. I really wasn't much of a coffee drinker, but it was a habit I had inherited from Momma. She never started her day without it.

John kept gazing at me, reading my every move and emotion. My brother had never been this serious with me. Most of the time we were playing, laughing and talking about all the things we went through as children. I'd remind him of the time Ms. Ruth slapped him at church, and he'd bring up the time Anna picked a fight with me at school. We never got tired of the teasing about the embarrassments we had tolerated.

He stared me directly in the eyes. "I think you know who killed Herman Camm."

I was astonished by his comment, compelled to walk out of my own kitchen. Herman Camm was a ghost. Just when I thought he was gone for good, something or somebody reminded me he did exist. His name continued to echo off my walls.

I turned to take a peek at Robert crawling on the floor. Then I said, "I don't know anything about his killer. The sheriff has already questioned me. Why are you bringing him up again?" For a quick moment, Robert's eyes appeared beady, just like those of his father. I batted my eyes and the image disappeared.

"Because it is a sore that will not heal for a lot of people in Jefferson County, I think it is an open wound for you, too. I also believe you know more than you are saying."

"Momma told you to stay away from Ms. Pearl."

"Pearl is being wrongly accused. If you know who did it, you need to speak up, Carrie."

"I don't know anything about it."

He sipped his coffee, still staring into my eyes, waiting for me to blink or move. Lawyers were like detectives. They had been trained in getting to the truth. But, there was no truth to get to. I didn't want to talk about Herman. Besides, he had gotten what he deserved. Abusers should be punished.

"I have spoken to a lot of people since I've been in Jefferson County. I even met Herman's brother, who is also searching for his killer."

I looked at him. "What do any of this have to do with me?"

"Carrie, Momma told me the entire story about you and Camm."

"There is nothing to tell. You say it like we had a love affair or something."

"I know what he did to you and if he had done that to me, I'd want revenge too."

"Do you think I killed him?"

"I'm not sure who did him in. I know I am sorry for what he did to you. I probably would have killed him myself if I had been home."

"There was not one thing nice about our stepfather. He was as close to a snake as anybody I knew. If you want to find his killer, you might start by having a candid talk with your client. Ms. Pearl knew him probably better than Momma. He was not the man we thought he was. He was not a good man, John." My eyes welled up and tears flowed from them.

John got up from the table and put his arm around my shoulder. "Sis, if you know what happened, please tell me."

I pulled away from him and shouted, "I don't know anything about his killer! How many times do I have to tell you this!?"

"Calm down."

"You've been in Jefferson for weeks now. Couldn't you find the killer? I'll answer for you. Nobody cared enough to tell."

"I talked to Jake, the bartender; Earl, his friend; the preacher and Ms. Pearl. All of them could account for their whereabouts. Pearl thought she did it, until they found him shot to death."

"Until he was shot to death . . . so that means she tried."

"The cuts were not deep enough to kill him. It was more like a deep scratch, according to the sheriff. We know a shotgun killed him."

"Why do you care who killed him, John?"

"I care now for the sake of my family. You and Simon could go to jail for this crime if the sheriff got his way."

"We didn't do it."

"Well, help me figure out who did."

I began by telling him how Mr. Camm treated me, how he followed behind me and made advances toward me whenever Momma was away. He listened intently, at times jotting down words on a writing tablet. I told him how I feared my own home, and then he asked, "Why didn't you tell somebody?"

"I couldn't. Remember how everyone treated Miss Topsie. The entire county turned against her, even the people at church. I didn't want that to happen to me."

"You had me."

"I know. I didn't know what to do. If I could live my life over, it would be different. No matter what happened, I didn't kill him."

"Did Simon do it?

"I don't think so," I answered, just as Simon walked through the door.

Before he spoke to me, he said, "John, what are you doing here?"

"I came by to see Carrie. I'm on my way back to D.C."

Simon kissed me on the forehead and reached down to pick up Robert who was playing on the floor.

"How long are you going to be here?"

"I'm leaving in an hour or so."

"You ought to at least stay for dinner."

Simon put Robert back down and pulled out a chair at the table. He went into the ice box and poured himself a glass of water. And then, he sat down.

John fumbled with his bow tie, adjusting it in a perfect line. He had always been a little finicky about his looks. He had often said, "Appearances are important." Afterward, he sipped his coffee, which was getting cold.

"Simon, what do you know about Camm's murder?"

"The cat got what he deserved," Simon declared. He hated it when people would bring up Herman Camm. He disliked the small talk as much as I did.

John paused for a moment. "Let me ask, did you do it? Did you kill him?"

Simon shook his head. "Hell, no! I didn't do it, but I wanted to. Somebody got to him before I could. That lowdown sucker had wronged a lot of people. Everybody in the damn town wanted him dead, including me."

"Jake at the bar said you stopped by the night he died."

"I was looking for him. But Jake claimed he was not in the place. I had the feeling Jake or Earl was covering up for him. So, I drove off."

"You sure you didn't do it."

"I looked for him that night. If I had found him, you wouldn't have recognized him. I would have beaten his ass to death. I was mad as hell. I drove around town, but no one knew where he was, so I left."

John listened, his eyes shifting from Simon to me. He was analyzing us, trying to figure out if we were telling the truth.

"If y'all didn't do it, then who did do it?" he asked in a serious tone.

I shook my head. Simon said, "When you hurt a lot of folk, anybody could be guilty of taking you out. Camm had a lot of enemies, so I hear."

"Who were they?" he asked.

"I thought you were a lawyer, not the sheriff. We don't know who wanted him dead. Furthermore, why do you care? What has Ms. Pearl done to you?" I raised my voice.

"I don't want my family to be charged and nobody is in Jefferson to defend them. The sheriff is not going to contact a lawyer on behalf of a colored man. I want him to leave my family members alone."

"Me too! Every time I go home, I expect to hear something about this murder. Camm is the only colored man ever to get this much attention. White folk don't care. The sheriff is just trying to find someone to hang."

John gazed at Simon. "Do you have anything else to say?"

Simon stared back. "Why don't you find the shotgun and then maybe you will find the killer. You done talked to the entire town already."

John put his writing pad back in his briefcase. Then his faced softened. He reached down and picked up Robert who was pulling up at his leg. "I've got to get going. Carrie, take good care of my nephew."

"Are you going to let this go?" I asked him.

"Yes, there is no reason for the sheriff to harass my family. I have to remember though, he is white."

CHAPTER 24

Mrs. Hall and I spent an entire day stringing popcorn and setting out red and white candles for the holiday. First, we put a wreath of pine cones and holly on the front door, and then put up, in our apartment, the cedar Christmas tree Simon brought home, and decorated it with popcorn, and a special stocking for little Robert. All down Broad Street ornaments and lights adorned the merchants' windows. It was exciting, and the brisk winter nights were luminous and bright. On some nights, we could hear the church bells ringing from a distance. It was festive. Even the horses and buggies going up and down the streets were decorated. My first Christmas away from home, and I wanted it to be special.

I invited everyone I knew to dinner including my friend Adam Murphy. I had run into him one day in the city. All week I had been thinking about him, wondering what he was doing, and if he had traveled back home to the Chesapeake area for the holiday. It was strange how he had remained in my thoughts. It was cold the day I saw him. He was walking down Broad Street alone, his collar turned up and a cap on his head.

"Carrie!" he shouted, as I turned the corner toward the children's store.

I knew the voice and a smile rippled across my face. It was a frigid day and I had been fighting the wind all the way down the street.

"I didn't think I would see you again," he said, grinning like I was funny-looking or something.

"Why are you looking like that?" I asked him, pulling my wool coat close to my body.

"I guess I'm happy to see you. How have you been doing?"

We stood close to the entryway of the building, letting the building shield us from the wind on all sides.

"I'm doing good," I said, watching the crowd dart in and out of the building, the cars parking and the horses and buggies trotting around the corner. With each step the horses took, the bells around the horses' necks rang. It was symmetry of trots and bells.

A gush of wind sent chills up my spine. I

started to shiver and my teeth chattered. The temperature, combined with the wind, was fierce. "Let's step inside out of the weather," I suggested.

Adam opened the door and we stepped inside. The first thing he said was, "I hope everything is working out for you and your husband."

"We're fine; how about you?" I asked him.

"I'm going to be here for the holiday. I can't afford to go home. I am working and I can't get off from work. You know the hotels never close." I remembered when he got that job. He had written me a letter with all the details.

"Where are you going for Christmas?"

"I'm going to try to make a pie at home," he said, smiling.

I suppose I was grinning too, since I had not seen him in over a month, almost two. He was my first school friend, and was instrumental in helping me find my way to school.

"Well, if you want to, you can come eat with us," I said before realizing it.

"I don't want to get you in any trouble. Your husband has already threatened me."

"He thought we had something going on then. Now he knows we were just good friends."

"Was that all, Carrie?" he asked.

I was a bit embarrassed by his comment, so guarded my tongue, trying not to open up too much. We were friends, but more.

"I had better finish shopping. I need to get back home."

He gazed at me, fixing his eyes directly on mine. It was scary, since I caught myself enjoying the connection.

"I've got to go," I said, breaking the stare.

His smile dissolved. "You take care of yourself." And in a blink, he turned and walked back into the wind.

I couldn't get him out of my thoughts the entire day. I purchased Robert a little wooden fire truck for Christmas and Simon some socks. It was all I could afford from the household cash jar. All the way home, I thought about the walks with Adam, about sitting on the steps of the administration building talking for hours, mainly about our dreams.

Before Robert was ever thought about, Simon and I would have long talks under the tree in the schoolhouse yard. We loved the time under the tree. We would kiss and hold hands and pretend like we were the only two people in the whole world. I loved the feeling. It was the same when I first came to Richmond. At night, we would lie in bed, Simon sharing his dreams of being a Negro Leaguer and scoring more runs than Pete Hill. Even though he still sent hot flashes through my body, there was something wrong. I felt he was keeping a secret from me. I was too afraid to inquire, not sure I really wanted to know what it was. I hoped it went away.

Mrs. Hall and I cooked Christmas Eve. She cooked the mashed potatoes, and I did the turkey, dressing, turnips and sweet potato pies. Instead of the light rolls Momma usually made, I did biscuits, something I knew how to cook.

Nadine came over with a cake she had baked. She was no guest of mine. However, she'd managed to plead to Mrs. Hall's emotion and she invited her and the children.

Mrs. Hall replaced her Northern sophistication and appeared to have embraced the Southern hospitality. It was Christmas Day. From the moment she opened the door, I could smell the aroma from the cedar Christmas tree, and the apple cider steaming on the stove. She had a smile from ear to ear. A white woman in an apron was a first for me. Every white woman I knew strolled around the house behind the help making sure there was no missing fine china or silver, and occasionally sliding a finger across the furniture searching for dust. But, for some odd reason, the whites trusted coloreds with their food. To me, food would have been the only way to get back at some of them for the insensitive and nasty ways white folks delivered to coloreds every day of their life. I even knew a few colored people who had laughed about adding a little pee or spit spice to the food before serving dinner. Ginny had said, "They would eat like it was the best-tasting food, and all I could do was smile inside. Now, I's know it was wrong, but at the time, I didn't care. I changed when they started asking me to take the leftovers home for dinner. I couldn't throw away good food, so I stopped adding the spice."

Little Robert's eyes danced at the sight of the people and food. Mrs. Hall had invited the entire community, it appeared: Nadine and her two children, the corner store merchant, Simon and me. I saw Nadine, and told myself to ignore her.

"Hey, Simon and Carrie!" Nadine shouted out.

"Merry Christmas!" Simon answered, and I waved.

"Have a seat," Nadine coaxed as if she was the woman of the house. I scanned the room for Jessie, and he was not around.

Mr. Hall was sitting at a table in the corner stacking dominoes in zigzag lines. Mrs. Hall was in the kitchen. Although the aroma was enticing, I worried about Mrs. Hall's ability to cook food. This was my first holiday away from Jefferson County. The last Christmas home had been painful. Momma had delivered Robert. She was stunned. *How could I be with child and she not know?* It is what happens when you stop paying attention to your own business. It was the night she found out Herman Camm had stolen my youth and her life.

Nadine scooted over on the davenport, patting the seat so I could sit down. I sat down beside her, but Simon didn't sit. Instead, he pulled a chair up at the card table, where Mr. Hall was stacking dominoes.

"You want to play?" Mr. Hall asked him.

"Why not? I might as well whip you while the evening is young."

"You sure talk a lot of shit for someone who is getting ready to get beat on Christmas Day." They both chuckled.

Mrs. Hall called from the kitchen, "Nadine, why don't you come in the kitchen?"

"I was going to sit here with Carrie. She looks like she could use a little company."

Her comment got underneath my skin. I

was all of a sudden shaking my leg like I did when my nerves were about to be rattled. Instead, I got up and went into the kitchen. I pulled out a chair at the kitchen table and watched as Mrs. Hall reheated the soda biscuits she'd asked me to make for the day.

Nadine followed me like a puppy and sat at the table. "You and Simon sort of look happy today," she said, crossing her legs and smoothing down her hair.

"We are happy," I replied. "This is our first holiday away from home."

"I enjoyed myself when we went to Jefferson. I can't cook like Mrs. Mae Lou, but we are still going to have a good time."

Nadine turned up her nose, and stared at the alabaster ceiling. "Y'all didn't ask me to go."

I ignored her comment. Then she added, "Simon probably would have a fit if I came."

"What do you mean?"

She shook her head. "He just wouldn't want me there."

Mrs. Hall interrupted her, "Nadine, how do you make gravy?"

Nadine smacked her lips. "Well, I usually brown some flour and add a little water."

"Mrs. Hall, I use the turkey drippings for seasoning," I chimed in.

"Believe it or not, I hardly ever cook a turkey. We usually eat a baked chicken and toast the holiday in with a glass of wine."

"That's 'cause y'all a little stuffy. People from up North always eat like that, like they are better," Nadine said.

Whatever truth she said, it didn't matter. It all sent a frustrating chill up my spine.

I didn't comment, even though I sensed inviting Nadine to our holiday get-together had the potential of turning sour.

Mrs. Hall took her time commenting, but when she did, she said, "No matter what is served, the point is it is Jesus' birthday. It is the reason we are here, and whether we serve turkey or ham, it really does not make a difference."

"You don't have to get your feathers ruffled. I feel peoples up North think they are better than us Southerners."

Now she had sparked a nerve in Mrs. Hall. When white folk get frightened or mad, they turn red. Mrs. Hall's face was pink, her pinky finger trembling. Nadine had an effect on most people, and it was nothing positive.

"Carrie, don't you think people up North think they are better than us?"

"Nadine, I really don't care. I am happy we all can come together to celebrate

Christ's birthday."

"I guess you right," Nadine said, and then added, "I suppose all peoples can get along if they try."

Nadine was what one of my professors at school called an antagonist. She was always trying to find someone to go up against, and this time, it was Mrs. Hall. To change the tone of the conversation, I volunteered to help set the table. The kitchen in Mrs. Hall's place was larger than mine. She had enough space for six people at the table, but with the children and adults, all of us could not eat at the same time. So, she and I made the children's plates first. We spooned out mashed potatoes, sliced turkey, gravy, green beans and yams.

While Nadine's two children ate their Christmas meal, I fed Robert potatoes and green beans. He loved smashed table food, and he smacked his mouth as if it was his first meal. In the front room, Nadine had maneuvered a wedge in between Mr. Hall and Simon. She now had the attention of both men, and especially Simon, who occasionally blushed at whatever was being said. I peered at her from the hallway with a squint in my eyes. She looked up and bent her head as to ignore me. After the children were finished eating, Mrs. Hall collected the soiled plates, stacked them in the sink and wiped her wet hands on a dish towel.

The children traded places with the adults and we all gathered around the table: Simon, the merchant from the corner, Mr. Hall and me. Just when Mr. Hall had asked us to sit down to eat, someone knocked hard on the door. Mr. Hall rushed to the front door. When he opened it, there was Adam Murphy. He stood smiling all wrapped up in a hat and scarf. It was cold. Everyone was expecting a white Christmas.

"Good evening, young man. I don't think I know you," Mr. Hall said, and waited for a response.

"I'm Adam. Carrie invited me to the Christmas dinner."

When I heard Adam's voice, I went to the door. He saw me and even a bigger smile blossomed across his face.

"Glad you could make it," I said. "We were just about to start dinner."

He took off his hat and coat and followed me into the kitchen, Mr. Hall right behind him.

When Simon saw Adam, his jaw twitched, but he didn't say anything. Strangely, Nadine was sitting next to him. I was on one side of Simon and Nadine on the other. Mr. Hall told Adam to have a seat across from me. Simon adjusted himself in his seat and reached over to shake Adam's hand.

"Welcome, Adam! It is Adam, right?" said Mrs. Hall.

"Yes, ma'am. Carrie invited me to dinner the other day. I hope it is okay."

"We have plenty of food."

I inhaled before I spoke. "Adam is one of my friends. We met when I was searching for a school. He is a student and can't go home for the holiday . . ."

"No need to explain. He is welcomed here," Mrs. Hall said, without hesitation.

Adam pulled out a seat and joined us at the table. Mrs. Hall passed a hot towel around so we could clean our hands. It was something new. We'd normally go to the washbowl and lather with lye soap, wipe our hands clean and eat.

After blessing the table for the second time, we began serving ourselves. Mr. Hall had blessed the table with the children just minutes before and had reminded them of the importance of celebrating Christmas; now he had done the same for the adults. For some reason, Simon held my hand especially tight, squeezing it. I don't know if it was Adam's presence or his love for me. However, it felt heartwarming.

"Adam," Simon said, "how long have you

been going to school around here?"

"I'm almost finished," Adam answered spooning out mashed potatoes and topping them with gravy.

"You plan on staying around here, or moving back home?"

"I haven't decided yet. I'm not sure if I'll be working with the pastor or teaching at a school."

"Do you have a woman?" Nadine asked him.

"No, I don't."

Nadine peeped around Simon at me. "I don't understand why a handsome man like you is still single."

Adam smiled. "I've got plenty of time to settle down."

"I know somebody must have your eye."

Adam glanced over at me. "Maybe," he said.

"Yeah, you need a good woman like I have," Simon interjected.

I smiled, knowing Simon had threatened Adam — told him to leave me alone.

Adam didn't comment. He continued with his meal, stuffing turkey and dressing on a fork.

Nadine had been smiling at Adam the entire meal. What started out as a flirtatious meal with Simon had become a get-to-know

Adam meal. She had glued her eyes to him, and was not going to move them. Mr. and Mrs. Hall appeared to enjoy the excitement of having people over for dinner. They took turns filling up our glasses with water and Bee's Knees, a popular drink of lemons, honey and gin.

"We must toast in the holiday. We have too much to be thankful for," Mrs. Hall said. And all of us held up our glasses and saluted the Christmas season. Adam reached across the table and tapped his glass with mine, our eyes met, and I discreetly looked the other way. It would have gone completely unnoticed if it hadn't been for Nadine.

"I want you to touch your glass with mine, just like you did Carrie's." I wanted to reach across Simon and yank her by the collar; instead, I put on my poker face and didn't murmur a word.

Adam reached across the table and touched his glass to hers. "This is especially for you, Ms. Nadine," he said. Nadine's smile ripped from ear to ear. I didn't like it.

Simon put his arms around my chair. It was as if he had something to prove. I was his wife, not Adam's; he had nothing to prove to me. The only thing I wanted to know was who was he hanging out with so much that Pearl and Nadine felt I needed to pay attention.

The meal was quite tasty, and sharing it with friends was so special for me. Little Robert was taking steps and pulling up and had managed to pull up using Adam's britches as an anchor. Adam reached down and picked him up. "Hey, big boy!" he said, smiling at Robert. Robert smiled and wiggled until he put him back on the floor. Simon looked concerned and his jaw tightened as it did when he was agitated.

The merchant told jokes about his patrons and all of us broke out in a hearty roar. The drink, Bee's Knees, had us all so relaxed we could barely stand. After dinner, while in a daze, I helped scrape the plates and assisted in washing the dishes. Nadine headed right back to the front room with the men and sat happily between Simon and Adam, her children sitting on the floor playing with Robert as if he were their Christmas doll baby.

Full of giggles, Nadine reached over and touched Adam on the leg. "You need to come see me sometime."

Simon listened with a smirk on his face, his eyes heavy from the drink the Halls had served.

Adam inhaled and bit his lip. He gently

moved Nadine's hand from his leg.

"What's wrong? You don't like girls." He didn't answer.

She put her hand back on his leg, and this time he didn't say anything.

"How do you like that?" Nadine had begun to unravel. She was loose.

"I know how to make a man feel real good," she said loud enough for us all to hear.

Finally, Simon said, "Nadine, you want a cup of coffee?"

"Hell, no! I want a man. You already taken and it look like Adam is for the taking."

"Calm down, Nadine," Simon attempted to persuade her.

"I just want to be nice. Simon, you know how nice I am."

Adam got up from the davenport. "Dinner was delicious, Mrs. Hall. Thank you for having me."

"You leaving, Adam?" Mrs. Hall asked.

"Yes, ma'am. The meal was the best. Thank you for opening your home up to me."

He got his coat and hat. Nadine said, "I live across the street. Stop by anytime." Then she proceeded to walk him to the door.

Before he left, he walked over to me and

kissed me on the cheek. "Merry Christmas, Carrie; thanks for inviting me." He shook Simon's and Mr. Hall's hands. I hated to see him leave, but it was getting late. Nadine followed him to the door. I wanted to tell her to sit down, but Simon was watching me like a hawk. The store owner walked out with Adam.

After the door was closed, Nadine came back in and sat beside Simon.

"I like him," she said, twirling her thick curls.

"Where's Jessie?" I asked.

In a slurred tongue, she answered, "I guess he is on a train somewhere. He supposed to be home in a few days."

Mrs. Hall glanced over at me. I shook my head, and sat down in the chair adjacent to the davenport. Mr. Hall had started working on his dominoes again.

"You know it has been a good day. I am so happy Adam and Mr. Scott could join us."

Mr. Hall got up and went over to her. "Merry Christmas, Darling!" he said. "I think this is the best holiday we've had in years. Carrie, Robert and Simon are like the family we always wanted."

"What about me?" Nadine said, "Me and my children need a family too."

"We are all family," Mrs. Hall commented, and Nadine's eyes lit up. Robert and the girls were on the floor playing. Each of the girls had a doll baby and Robert had a little wooden train. The children were as happy as we were. When we finally decided it was time to go home, the Halls asked us to let Robert stay the night with them.

"Children make the holiday worth it all," Mr. Hall said.

"So I guess it is time for me to leave too," Nadine said, standing up in front of Simon as if she was waiting for him to ask her to move.

"It is time for us all to call it a night," Simon replied, scooting around Nadine.

She peered at me. "I wonder if that Adam Murphy is alone tonight."

I bit my lip.

"I think he's got a thing for you, Carrie," Nadine remarked.

"No, not at all."

Nadine turned toward Simon. "You better watch them two."

"Nadine, please stop it! You need to go on home. The Bee's Knees is doing the talking," said Simon.

"I'm not drunk. I feel good. Come on, children; let's go home." She hugged the Halls. Then she said to Simon, "I would kiss you, but your wife is looking." She turned and threw a kiss. I wasn't sure if it was for me, however, I was certain it was for Simon.

We followed her out of the door. We went up the stairs to our apartment. The moon was high and the snow was beginning to fall.

CHAPTER 25

Richmond, Virginia, was a beautiful place, especially during the holidays. The bells on the horses and buggies rang out with each trot of the horse. The choir from the neighborhood church caroled throughout the community. Colored folk appeared to be happy in spite of that across the railroad tracks, the white people were looking down their noses at them, expecting them to serve their meals and clean the homes. I was glad we had our own neighborhood. It was like a private planet for us coloreds. We had our own schools, stores and merchants. I could find everything I needed in my own community. The winter vacation from school had been a good break. Simon had been home for more than a month. This was unusual. I had to get up to feed the baby, cook the breakfast and see about the two people I loved the most.

Now I was back in Petersburg. The start

of the semester left me feeling guilty for leaving Robert and his daddy at home. Women were supposed to be housewives. "A woman should be home taking care of the family," Momma told me in a letter she had written me. *Why were people so old-fashioned? It was the 1920s after all.* Most of the women I knew put the needs of their men before their own needs. I was raised to do the same, but for some reason, I couldn't do it.

My roommates and I had become good friends. One of them in particular was a lot like me. She was a country girl and she was making her own way. Ethel Coates was from Petersburg, but her family lived on the outskirts of town on a small farm. And, like me, Ethel experienced the guilt of leaving home. Her parents wanted her to stay home and watch her siblings while they worked, and she rebelled and enrolled in school. They did not support it. As with many uneducated families, home was more important than education. We had just learned about George Washington Carver who believed that good farming and agriculture began with education.

We had been back in school two weeks before Adam Murphy took the train down for a visit. He surprised me the same evening an old man who worked at the rooming house decided to make a pass at me. Ethel had warned me about him, "You know that old man is mighty mischievous. He is always watching me."

"He's never looked at me at all, and I am glad."

"I would never want to be alone with him," she said, shaking her head in disgust.

The man, Mr. Pete, we called him, was there only a couple of days a week. Usually he kept the grass low and fixed things up around the house. He shoveled coal into the furnace and made sure the winter garden of cabbage, kale, turnips and collards was weeded. He was a quiet man, short and partially bald. He reminded me of my grandpa.

But one day, after dinner was over and I was washing the dishes, which was how I paid my boarding, he tried to touch me on the bottom. All of a sudden, I was back in the place I had been with Mr. Camm. First fear and then anger came over me, especially when he pushed me in the corner. I had made a mental vow to never let anyone take advantage of me again. So, I yelled to the top of my lungs. Ethel came running down the stairs. When she got to the kitchen, I had a knife on Mr. Pete. "Please don't kill him, Carrie," Ethel pleaded.

"I didn't mean it," Mr. Pete stuttered.

I didn't move. I was determined that what had happened with Mr. Camm would never happen to me again. I felt the sweat sliding down my face, my chest heaving and my breath panting. I was angry and scared all at once. I didn't know I had the knife at Mr. Pete's neck. I had lost it.

When I backed off of Mr. Pete, he started to cry. "I wasn't gonna hurt you."

"You are a liar," I heard myself say.

"Get out of here, Mr. Pete!" Ethel yelled, and pushed him from behind. It was at that moment I felt liberated. I had more power than I thought. After awhile, the tears rolled down my face. I asked myself, *Why didn't you stop Mr. Camm?* The only answer I could think of was that now I didn't have anything to lose. What my momma or the church members thought no longer mattered.

Adam's visit was timely. Together Ethel and I told our story to the landlady, and she didn't hesitate to tell Mr. Pete to find another job.

The same night I told Adam about Robert and how Simon had been the love of my life.

"So, does that change things between us?"

he asked me in the library, and waited patiently for me to give him an answer.

I shrugged my shoulders, struggled with my words, found myself questioning my relationship with Adam. I enjoyed Adam in my life. He was a friend. And it was not a good thing for married women to be seen with single men, but I didn't want him to leave. "I wanted you to know the real me."

He kissed me on the cheek. "I know you are good, Carrie. You are beautiful to me."

What he said made me nervous. Perhaps I was leading him on or had I replaced Simon with Adam? I wasn't sure.

"I think it is time for me to go back to the house."

Adam put on his coat. Then he helped me with my wrap and scarf. We left the small library filled with shelves of books by mainly white people and a few by coloreds Booker T. Washington, George Washington Carver, and Paul Lawrence Dunbar. As we vacated the room filled with books, I pondered over the thought that if books could talk, what would they say?

When we got back to the house, Adam didn't want to go. "It is still early," he said after pulling out his pocket watch, reading it, and putting it back in his front pocket.

"It is nearly eight o'clock. We have a ten

o'clock curfew on the weekends."

"Can I come in?" he asked with a begging face.

"I guess you can for a little while," I said, opening the door.

In the sitting area were two couples, one of them holding hands so tightly, it seemed as if they could not let go, and the other in chairs facing each other and staring. Neither of them seemed to notice us when we entered the room. We sat at the table in the corner of the room. It was a large room. We used it for about everything. It was the parlor, our study area and where we received guests. It was a Victorian-style room, with colonial furniture and a fireplace that was lit and shooting out kindling sparks. It was warm, and when I saw the other couples, I wondered about Simon, who had a car and could easily come visit me, but hadn't.

We decided to play a popular game, one I'd learned from my primary teacher. We took out a sheet of writing paper, and made double crosses on it. It was something we did to kill time. So Adam chose an "O" and I used the "X." He said, " 'O' is for you. A complete circle, because you complete me."

"Well, I guess the 'X' symbolizes us doing wrong."

He frowned. "No, 'X' symbolizes the truth."

We played Tic-tac-toe until our eyes were heavy. All the time, I noticed Adam gazing at me differently, like he knew me and could tell things about me. His past seemed flawless and pure, but there was something he wanted to say.

"What is wrong with you?" I asked him.

"All this time I've been thinking about you, hoping one day you would leave Simon and then I could make my move. Now you tell me the entire story and now I don't want to wait. Simon is a good man, but you are a better woman. He doesn't understand you like I do."

I sort of felt uncomfortable. "What do you mean, Adam? Simon knows me. We are from the same place. Everybody at home knows us."

"That's not what I'm talking about," he whispered.

Nobody was listening. The other couples in the room were occupied with each other. One of the couples was kissing passionately on the lips, and the other squeezing hands. Both of them so hypnotized in each other's presence, they didn't notice or care about our conversation.

Adam cleared his throat. "Listen, we both

want the same thing. We both enjoy dream-
ing. We see education as a way out. Your
husband finds his freedom in taking
chances, like playing baseball or hustling at
the club. You and me," he pointed, "we are
the same."

I thought about what he said, yet it was
not convincing to me. I liked Adam, and
enjoyed the attention he gave me, yet I
wasn't sure he was mature enough to take
on the enormous responsibility which came
with loving a girl like me. Simon had from
the beginning. Besides, I was a married
woman.

I noticed the vulnerability in his eyes from
across the table. He was peering at me with
a certain intensity that was hard to explain,
his eyes serious, and his hand across the
table gripping mine like he didn't want to
let go. We were having a special moment,
and neither of us could envision where it
would lead.

Strange thoughts came into my mind.
"Can we stop talking about these things? It
is wrong, Adam."

He squeezed my hand tighter. "Can you
please stop worrying about what is right, for
Christ's sake, and think about what is
good?"

I stood up. "I don't know what is good."

"You know, and so do I."

I handed him his hat and scarf from the coat hanger. "It is getting late; my curfew is almost over."

"Come on, Carrie, we can do it," he said, as we walked to the door, his face glowing with anxiety as if I were going to give in at that moment.

"You've got to leave; my time is almost up."

With the front door wide open, he pulled me in and kissed me fervently. I closed my eyes, embarrassed by my reaction. I held him tight, knowing it was all wrong. Afterward, I watched him walk toward the colored section of town and then out of sight into the trees. I wanted to run after him and pull him back into my arms. I longed for Adam for days after he left.

CHAPTER 26

Because Simon was in town, I didn't travel home as frequently. And it puzzled me why Simon hadn't bothered to make the thirty-minute drive to Petersburg to visit me. I hadn't seen him in three weeks. So on Thursday, right after my history class ended, I packed and went straight to the train depot.

I had an eerie feeling when I arrived at the depot. A chill rushed over me as often happened when I sensed trouble. Nadine's man, Jessie, watched me with an eagle's eye like always. This time, he had more nerve — like he had to make something happen when he approached me, grinning. "You are going home early this week, huh?"

"I've been in school for three weeks now; my little boy is probably walking all over the place," I said and sat down in the last seat in the colored section.

"Well, you look pretty," he said.

"Thank you," I replied, blushing a little at the compliment, which would have made Nadine angry as a wild dog.

Ever since Jessie had moved back in with Nadine and the children, she had been quiet. She had not approached me one time about Simon, and she had stopped asking about Adam. She seemed content and happy again. I would see Jessie, Nadine and the children walking up the street. She and Jessie were holding hands and the children were smiling like Cheshire cats. Nadine's bitterness toward Simon and me had finally dissolved. So, I knew Jessie was coming on to me in an attempt to make her jealous, or to test himself, since he had gone back to the woman he said was no good.

"It's a shame your husband lets you come down here all by your lonesome self," he said.

I bit my lip. "I'm okay. I'm in school surrounded by a lot of girls trying to become teachers. I'm not alone."

He stood there gazing at me with an inquisitive stare. "I still don't understand how Simon could let you come down here as pretty as you are."

I did not comment and he didn't move, stood there peering down on me, scanning my body like it belonged to him. When the train started to move, he turned and walked back to his station and stood there like a soldier guarding his territory.

I glanced up and he was still looking at me, so I focused my attention out of the window at a man in a buggy with canisters filled with the fresh milk he was selling.

For some reason, the trip home seemed longer than before. We stopped at every depot along the twenty-mile run. Along the route, two domestic workers got on the train and a man who made me shake in my seat. The man was the spitting image of Herman Camm. Immediately, my chest started to heave, and I felt nervous all over, my leg shaking like a leaf.

The man, dressed in a gray suit and hat, did not see me. He sat in the front of the train's car and I sat in the back. He didn't turn around and I squirmed, fearfully, in my seat. I held my head down and prayed he didn't look my way. My knees were shaking and I was suddenly hot.

Jessie walked over to me. "You look like something is wrong. Are you all right?" he asked.

"I'm okay," I answered him, trembling all over.

"You sure you are okay?" he asked again.

"Yes," I said quickly. I didn't want him

298

standing over me inviting any attention from the stranger in the front of the train.

"Let me know if you need anything." He walked to the front of the car, which was coming to a halt at another stop.

Just before we made it into Richmond, the stranger got up and got off the train. As the train passed the stranger walking along the tracks, my eyes nearly popped out of my head when the man turned and peered over at me. It was Herman Camm!

I wasn't sure he recognized me because I had pulled my scarf up around my neck. He could only see my eyes. He didn't react and as the train kept moving along the track, I wondered who that man could be. I couldn't help breathing hard, as if I had just run a race. I told myself my eyes were playing tricks on me. There was no way a dead man could come back to life.

When the evening train finally stopped, I got off, waved at Jessie and headed back to Jackson Heights where I lived. As I crossed over Broad Street, I thought about Adam. I wanted to stop, but all at once, I was too fearful to go in the direction of his apartment. The Model Ts and Studebakers had almost replaced the buggies in the city, so the traffic was faster than ever before. I crossed the street and was nearly hit by a car making a sharp right turn. The loud horn got my attention. The thought of the resurrection of Mr. Camm had me numb.

There was a chill in the air. People were wrapped up fending off the winter wind. No matter how cold it was, I was sweating under my coat. I reached the place where the streets split and walked past the nightclub, the homemade ice cream shop, and the corner store. I was no longer concerned about the man I thought was Mr. Camm; the entire time I was convincing myself he was dead and six feet under.

When I made it to our apartment, I still could not shake that strange feeling. I didn't stop at the Halls since Simon had been caring for Robert. I knew he was home. His black Model T was parked in front of the house and shining like new money. I opened the door, which was always unlocked except at night when the latch was hooked securely. Sitting at the kitchen table sipping on a glass of elderberry wine was Nadine, her hair out of place and her white collared blouse unbuttoned all the way down to the cleavage. She glanced up and saw me and immediately grabbed her blouse and buttoned back the unhooked buttons to the top. "I just got here," she said immediately, her eyes wide open, and gazing toward the bedroom door.

All of a sudden, my fear was replaced with anger. "Why are you in my house?"

"I just stopped by for a minute."

"Why are you here?" I asked.

At that moment, Simon came out the bedroom and into the kitchen. He had on his undershirt and a pair of trousers. He always took his shirt off just before bed. He bit his bottom lip and a frown of concern took over his face. "When did you get here?"

I could feel the warmth spread all over my body, and I was shaking "What is she doing here?"

He started to stumble. "Nadine just stopped by for a drink. We were just talking."

"A drink?" I asked, my eyes squinting into slits, anger rising in a rush.

"Yeah, she just came across the street, right, Nadine?" Nadine's face was expressionless and her eyes fearful.

I rolled my eyes toward Nadine. "Get out!" I yelled. "I ought to tell Jessie about you. You no-good floozy!"

She picked up the glass of wine and gulped it down like an alcoholic, so quickly most would choke. "Now we wasn't doing nothing, Carrie," she nervously explained, holding her hand in front of her to keep me from slapping her face.

"Get out!" I screamed at the top of my voice, my hands trembling.

Simon walked over to me, and threw up his hands as he explained, "We were just having a drink, nothing else, I promise you."

I wanted to rip his T-shirt off and beat him in the chest.

"We were just spending a little time together, Carrie. You been gone and he was lonely," Nadine added.

"Shut up!" Simon demanded and gave Nadine a cold stare. She sucked her teeth and bit her lip. "Go home, Nadine!" he yelled.

Nadine grabbed her coat with so much force, she almost fell. I walked over to her and shoved her in the back, pushing her across the floor. "Get yo hands off me," she warned me, swinging her arms in disgust.

"Get out!" I shouted again and opened the door. Then I shoved her as hard as I could out onto the porch.

After I slammed the door closed, I asked Simon, "Where's Robert?"

"He is downstairs," Simon said, sweating with worry, watching me — reading me, wondering what I would do next.

"I'm going to get him," I said, "and when

I get back, I want you out of here." I turned to walk away.

He shouted, "I ain't going nowhere! You hear me, Carrie!?"

I threw my head up and walked out of the door with speed I didn't know existed. I went down the stairs to the Halls, and stopped just before knocking. Cold tears streamed down my cheeks. I wiped them with the back of my hand. inhaled and gathered my composure. Then, I knocked on the door.

Mrs. Hall knew what was going on, yet she didn't mutter a word. I took Robert in my arms and went home.

Simon was still there when I came back. He made an effort to talk, but I couldn't speak — at the time I couldn't stand him. I just wanted to hold my son, and tell him I loved him. Robert glanced up at me and smiled. His smile helped remove the agitation and anger I had just experienced.

All evening Simon followed me around. "Can we talk about what you think happened?"

"No, not at all, and not right now," I said, as I got Robert ready for bed.

It had been a disruptive and stressful day. From the minute I saw a man who looked like Camm, to seeing Nadine at my kitchen table, it was all more than I could handle alone. I poured myself a glass of wine, and stared out the front-room window. It was a clear night and my husband was staring at me, waiting for me to crawl into bed. So he wanted *to talk,* I thought. Is that what he and Nadine had been doing?

"Simon, you can sleep right there on the davenport!" I said and went into the bedroom. I pulled the sheets off my bed and put on clean ones.

"You are my wife. I'm not sleeping anywhere but beside you!" he yelled back at me. I rolled my eyes and continued to change the bedding. Simon followed me.

He pleaded, "I don't want Nadine. I was just having a little drink with her before I hit the road again. I miss you, Carrie."

"You are a hopeless liar. You and Nadine can be together for all I care."

He grabbed me and pulled me close. "I want you," he said. All the time I could smell the stench of Nadine on his body.

"I can't believe a word you say. Seems like you've had all of the females in the club . . ."

"Where did you get that from? I ain't been with none of them bitches."

"I thought you were out playing ball with the league. You have been seen all over Richmond."

Simon was without words. He stared at me wondering where I was getting my information. "Who is telling you this stuff?" I watched him pace the floor back and forth. "Somebody is telling lies on me," he said, sitting down on the davenport and knowing he was not going to sleep in my bed.

CHAPTER 27

It was on a trip back to Petersburg that I was finally able to have a talk with Simon. The weeks Simon had been away — traveling up and down the coast of Virginia and Maryland with a local team didn't leave much time for serious conversations. He had moved from the outfield to first base. He knew if he shined and outplayed a few of the stars, he would definitely find a permanent place on the newly forming Eastern Colored League. It had been rumored the teams would be in place in the next two years. After a long weekend, Simon drove me back to school. We were cordial; however, I had not forgiven him for his indiscretion with Nadine.

As we drove down the street past the nightclub where Ms. Pearl was singing, Simon almost drove onto the cobblestone sidewalk, just missing a man walking down the street. He got my attention! I held onto the dashboard, afraid we were going to wreck and tumble over. "Did you see that man?!" he shouted in disbelief.

I was afraid to blink my eyes. It was the same man I'd seen on the train, standing in front of the nightclub as if he were waiting and watching for someone. "I saw him," I said. He was well dressed in a brown suit with a Stetson cocked over one eye — the same style of dress as Mr. Camm.

Stunned, Simon took a left turn and drove around the corner and back to the night-club. "You don't sound surprised," he said, while glancing from side to side looking for the man we had just seen.

"I'm not, Simon. I saw him on the train when I came home a month ago. I thought it was my mind playing tricks on me."

"Why didn't you say something?"

"I was going to tell you the day I found Nadine in my house. So, you know how that went."

Simon reached over and grabbed my hand, and then he put on the brakes and slowed the car down. He waited impatiently for a buggy to cross in front of the car. "Go, go, go," he said. It slowed him to a near stop. As he cruised around the corner, he checked on each side of the street. He wanted to get a good view. When we rode

307

past the nightclub, the man was no longer there. He had escaped once again.

Simon pounded his fist on the dashboard. "That son of a bitch is supposed to be dead," he said. "I saw him laid out in the casket."

"What is going on?" I said, shaking my head from side to side remembering the murder, investigation and more upsetting, the rape.

"I don't know, but once I get back in town tonight, I'm gonna find out."

Simon's eyes turned dark as night as we drove down the road toward Petersburg, a permanent frown line between his eyebrows. We both were curious, and I was scared to death. For three weeks I had been walking around campus concerned I might run into Herman. I had told Ethel the story and she'd warned me, "You are paranoid." I had to look the word up in the dictionary.

"Maybe a little," I'd answered. What was more suspicious than the handling of my fear was the mysterious question on my mind. Wasn't Herman Camm supposed to be dead?

"Be careful, Simon; we don't want any trouble," I said.

"It is puzzling the man is lurking around the club. He must have some type of business there. My guess is Ms. Pearl is his business."

"Herman Camm is dead, Simon. We don't know who the man was standing there."

"I'm definitely going to find out."

When he put me off in front of the rooming house, he warned me, "Be careful. I will pick you up on Friday, so do not go near the train depot. Stay close to the rooming house, and don't walk alone," Simon directed me, and drove off as fast as he could.

After dealing with the worker at the house, I would never let another man take advantage of me.

Studying had kept me busy most of the time. As the classes became more advanced, I stayed up later at night. I found myself lighting the kerosene lamp in an attempt to read all the requirements for an educator. I loved to read, but there were several things interrupting my sleep. Thinking about Mr. Camm being alive was crazy. And times when I longed for Simon's gentle touch, a vision of Nadine sitting in my kitchen, kept me awake and jittery. I had a lot of things going on inside of me.

Things changed the night Adam dropped by for a visit on his way to his cousin's house in the bottom. Ethel had her eye on him, had noticed him the first time he'd visited me at school. She'd said, "He seem to be a nice man." And she blushed. But, for some reason, Adam had not noticed her at all. He shrugged her off several times, sending her away with a sad face and wondering if she'd been too forward with him. I told her there were many more men to choose from; he was probably already taken. "But, wouldn't you know about it?" she asked.

"Not really," I answered. "We don't talk about that subject."

Adam Murphy came to visit me on the Wednesday after Simon dropped me off. A blanket of February snow covered the trees. It was a quiet evening, the moon was high, and the reflection on the snow made the air feel romantic. Our footprints disappeared as we walked from the small library to the rooming house. Just before we made it to the house, Adam invited me to stop at a room he had rented for the night. It was unusual for him to pay for a place to stay when he had family down in the bottom.

"Let me show you where I am staying tonight," he said, smiling. We climbed several stairs toward an apartment around the back of a two-story house. It was around the corner from the school. It was a wretched little place. The stench of it being closed up made me feel sick. We opened the window and the scent dissipated. The freshness of the bed linen replaced the stale air. Along with the bed was a desk and washbowl. Everything was plain. What puzzled me was Adam staying there. "Why are you here instead of at your cousin's?" I asked as I sat down in the chair at the desk.

"This is my only means of being close to you," he said jokingly. However, the lines around his eyes and the seriousness of his posture were indications of business. I liked what I knew about him. His disposition of kindness was always the same.

"We've had this talk before, Adam. I am married," I said, gazing directly in his eyes.

He did not hesitate to comment. "I know you are married, but I hope not for long. I have my own plans for us."

"Your friendship is important to me. I don't want to destroy what we have."

"What do you mean?"

"I am married. I don't believe in doing wrong. I've been raised right."

He shook his head. "You are not crazy. You are a student at a good school. Soon you will be a teacher. Are you going to stick around while your husband runs around with other women? What kind of lesson is that going to be?"

I stood up. "Adam, I think you are wrong. You don't know anything about Simon. He's really a responsible man."

"He is out there, Carrie, and you are too naïve to see it. He is not home with you and Robert. He is chasing his dreams and women."

"They don't mean anything to him."

He reached over and grabbed my hand. "Can you at least think about it? I know you have feelings for me. I can see it in your eyes. You are just trying to do right. Everybody can't do right because the world will not let them. When you get tired of him, I'll be right here."

"Are you moving to Petersburg?"

"No, I just wanted to spend some time alone with you. I didn't want to whisper at the rooming house, and I didn't want your friend Ethel thinking I wanted her — young women can get the wrong impression — even though she is beautiful. Now take us, Carrie, we are good for one another," he said, breaking a subtle smile, and I sat back down and gazed at him intently.

We stared each other in the eyes. Adam's dark eyes, serious and focused, made me jittery, since I didn't know how deep my feelings were for him. I was unable to figure out what he really meant to me.

"You deserve better than Simon. You are a special kind of woman, and I want to be a part of your life."

"I know, Adam. I've enjoyed your company too."

Adam had one of the most vulnerable looks on his face, but I could not give in.

"It's getting late," I said. The kerosene lamp's flickering gave the room a sultry feel even in the heart of winter. Adam asked me to sit on the bed beside him. I did, but said I had to leave.

"Don't go," he pleaded and then pulled me close and kissed me passionately on the lips. It felt good. I lay down beside him and faced the wall. He put his arms around my waist and pulled up close to me, his breath warming my neck. I wanted to scream "stop," but couldn't. I felt my body twitching and the warmth rushing all over me. Just his touch caused me to be weak. From behind me, I could feel the stiffness of his manhood. The sweat trickled down my face and the moisture dripped from my body. I wanted to love him. I loved the way he loved on me, how he started from my head and ended with my toes. He ran his fingers across my nipples and then down my side and inside my thighs. I wanted to let go — give in to him, and so did my body. When he began to part my thighs, I couldn't think of anything but him. Nadine and Simon had been forgotten.

After going back to my room, it wasn't long before my conversation with Simon re-appeared in my mind.

"You are my wife," Simon had mumbled.

"I know you've been sleeping with Nadine. I am not a fool."

"Nadine is not my wife."

"What is she then?"

"She is nobody to me," he'd said.

Now, I thought to myself, Adam was more than a friend to me.

CHAPTER 28

The weekend Simon picked me up, John showed up at our house. He came with an interrogating grimace on his face, somewhat like the one he'd had the last time he paid us a visit. This time he was ready and it was evident by the look in his eyes. Simon and I were home. We had just finished a hearty breakfast of spiced sausage, eggs and biscuits.

"You want something to eat?" I asked him.

"Just coffee will be fine," he said in a firm tone, as he took a seat at the kitchen table, and opened his briefcase.

"What brings you here today?" I asked, serving him the coffee.

He added a cube of sugar and stirred it, and then took a sip of it. "We need to talk."

"What's on your mind?" I had wondered that when I'd opened the front door and saw him standing there with his briefcase in his hand.

"I know who the killer is."

Simon and I didn't react. We watched him swallow and place his cup onto the saucer. Neither of us commented.

"Did you hear me?" he asked.

"Yes, we heard you. Who is the killer?" I was afraid it was Simon since he did not move. He sat still with a serious stare in his eyes and listened without flinching.

Finally, Simon said, "John, are you accusing us of killing Camm? If so, I've got some news for you."

John got up without waiting for me and poured another cup of coffee. He added sugar and cream to it and sat back down. "No. I've been talking to some folks all over Jefferson County. I have been to the joint and talked to every one of Camm's associates."

"Why, John, is it so important to find who killed Camm? Why are you trying to do a job the sheriff can do all by himself? We are getting over him. I don't want to keep talking about him. None of this is good."

He shifted himself and got up from the kitchen table. He walked over to the kitchen window and peered out of it. He was no longer the country John, wearing bib overalls. He was more city than ever. His shoes were shining and the cuffs of his pants were creased. He paused for a few seconds. "Because I want to free my family from it all. The people in Jefferson respect us; our papa was a fine man. It is my duty to put this murder to rest. The sheriff is a dumb boy. He is not smart enough to be in the job, but he's a white boy and that's all that matters in this country. I want to clear the Parker name and move on."

"The sheriff is not going to like you messing in his business."

He sat back down. "I did it for us, not the damn sheriff. We need our good name cleared. This man has left dirt in our path, and now it is time we clear it all up."

Simon was getting a bit concerned. He had studied John from top to bottom, as he always did when he was trying to figure out someone's intentions. "So, John, what did you find out? Who killed the son-of-a-bitch?"

"I'm not so sure he is dead," I said.

"He is dead all right. He is dead," John stated.

"Well, why is there a man walking around town looking just like him?"

He didn't flinch, didn't show any emotion. He knew the fellow. "The man you've seen is his brother. Camm had a twin."

"What?" Simon and I both said at the

same time.

It explained the train trip and the man in front of the club. But, why did he all of a sudden show up? We were spending days and months on Camm's murder, and what about poor Willie? Did anyone care about an upright man?

"Herman's brother has been around town looking for his brother's killer. He and I teamed up in Jefferson over a month ago. We talked to a lot of cats and I ended up back at home, Carrie."

"What are you saying?"

"Earl, one of Herman's best friends went over the night again with me."

Simon pulled himself up high in the chair to give the conversation his full attention. I inhaled and waited.

"The night Herman was killed, a lot of people were looking for him. Simon, you were there too. They said you seemed mad enough to kill anybody."

Simon folded his arms, his facial muscles flexing. "Listen, I don't care what those people say."

"Wait, before you get bent out of shape, they saw you drive off. So nobody is concerned about you killing the man. I was just telling the story."

Simon didn't say a word, only stared at

John like he was the enemy.

"It's going to be all right," I said to Simon, and tapped him on the arm. He gazed at me with soft eyes, and everyone seemed to relax.

John even eased up. "Well, Earl said Camm had wronged a lot of people. He'd been seeing another woman." Then he interjected, "Momma didn't know about it at first."

"I don't know why she didn't; he was always away from home. He would leave sometimes and wouldn't return until the next day. I can remember Momma opening the door in the early morning hours helping him to her bed."

"She really didn't know," John added. There are a lot of things we didn't know about this man. We didn't know about Ms. Pearl. Ms. Pearl had known him for years before he even knew Momma. In the meantime, he was causing problems for a lot of people. Still, no one had the right to take his life."

Simon's eyes narrowed at the discussion of Herman Camm. It was obvious the mention of his name was irritating to him. I was not the only one wondering why his ghost was still around.

"Can you just tell us who killed the

dude?" he urged John.

John cleared his throat, annoyed by Simon's frustration. "I have narrowed it down to our family."

My eyes flew open, and I gasped in fear. "Let me ask you a question, Carrie," he said, gazing at me in a fixed stare. I inhaled and felt my heartbeat thumping under my clothes.

Before I could say anything, Simon said, "She's your sister, John; leave her alone."

"I'm not accusing her of anything," he quickly shot back.

"Carrie, did you see Carl the night Herman Camm was killed?"

All of a sudden my memory began to fail me. "I don't know. He was at home," I said, not knowing if he was home or not. Since he did not go to joints and places like that, I was pretty sure he was home with Mary.

"I asked the same question to Momma and the both of them started shaking uncontrollably."

"Did you know, Simon, that Camm had made a pass towards your sister?"

"If he had, she would have said something to me."

John got up and moved around the circumference of the room. He peered at Simon. "Why would she tell you when she has a husband?"

"Listen, John, I don't know where you are getting this from, but who the hell is the murderer?"

"Camm made advances to Mary and she told Carl the same day he was murdered. He had access to the house and to Momma's rifle. He could have killed him and nobody would know."

I got angry. "Leave it alone, John. Let this rest."

"I want everybody in the family to know where my investigation ended. I don't want Kindred, Camm's brother, to know anything about this."

"You are the one talking to him."

"I had no choice. I led him in another direction because for some reason, I think he knows it was Carl."

Simon said, "Carl ain't kill nobody."

"I hope not, but if he did, please don't let Kindred know about it."

I bit my lip and shook my head because I knew about him making an advance on Mary, but I didn't think Carl knew. I did know he would use the rifle behind Momma's door often, especially when he was hunting rabbits.

When John left, he told us to never talk about this again, especially to anyone outside of the immediate family. "What do you know about Herman's brother?" Simon inquired.

"I don't know much about him, but as strange as it might seem, he is the spitting image of his brother; his height and weight are about the same. The only thing missing is the stench of liquor. He even walks and talks like him. They are identical in all ways. I've never seen twins with so many features alike."

Simon glanced over at me. Neither of us commented.

John seemed to be distrusting of his own words. He didn't stop with a comment about being identical, but added more to think about, "The only difference is that Kindred don't go into joints like Herman. He is a saved man."

CHAPTER 29

Ms. Pearl had taken up with Herman Camm's brother. It was one of those things which had the folk in Jefferson whispering again. Momma wrote me about it, but I had seen her myself with him. People had seen them together at church in Jefferson and on the streets in Richmond. They were a couple. The sheriff told Ginny there was no way Pearl Brown could have committed the murder since she was spending time with the brother. Once again, the investigation was put off. Most people knew the sheriff was not smart enough to catch a killer. He had been friends with a man who killed his wife. He thought she had drunk the lye on her own. He finally realized he was wrong about the husband after someone else pointed it out to him. *Who can stand to drink lye?* Why was there so much concern about Herman, when Willie was murdered too? Everybody had figured out it was the white man, so no one mumbled a word about it.

Simon and I ran into Adam Murphy at the nightclub in Jackson Heights. He was holding hands with a beautiful lady around his age. He saw me and walked over to me pulling the lady with him. Simon recognized them and a smirk came to his face.

Adam hugged me. "It is so nice to see you."

"You too," I responded.

Simon reached out and shook his hand. Adam seemed a bit annoyed; immediately the smile on his face disappeared. After shaking Simon's hand, he turned toward his date and they went hand in hand to a table in the middle of the room, not far from the one where we were sitting. The sight of him with another woman at first bothered me. Why? I couldn't understand. Seeing him happy was something I'd wanted for him. Adam was a decent man, inspiring me in any endeavor I took on. It was important to have support when women's rights were still being challenged. The Women's Suffrage March had taken place less than ten years before, so anything positive for women leaving the house I counted as special.

Ms. Pearl had been dazzling the crowd for weeks. A sellout crowd had been heightening the reputation of the club that had to live down a murder. At first, after it had happened, no one could pay patrons to stop by. No one wanted to be associated with a tarnished location. It was Willie who had loss his life to a white man's bullet and nobody cared. Now, Ms. Pearl was back and many of Jackson Heights elite were all dressed up and in the club. Ms. Walker emerged after declaring months ago she would not step into the establishment again until the owner made a declaration that the club was violence free.

It was cool outside, yet inside, it was starting to get hot. After sitting down, I panned the room. I peered in the direction of Adam and he was looking my way.

Simon tapped me on the shoulder, "Are you all right?"

"This is my first time coming to hear Ms. Pearl sing since Willie was murdered."

"You see the big men standing over in the corners. They are there to keep order. I helped find them," Simon boasted.

When I saw the two big men weighing over 250 pounds and standing at least six feet, four inches tall, all of the tension I'd built up inside began to soften. The thought of bullets flying around had many people wondering what might happen. Mrs. Hall even warned us to stay alert. "Y'all pay attention in a place like that and never sit with your back toward the entrance. You need to see who is coming and going." I felt it was good information coming from her, since most of her life she had been under scrutiny. Then I wondered what she really knew about places like the club.

Out of the corner of my eye, I noticed Nadine walking toward us. I wanted to get up and leave, but it was too late, "How y'all doing?" she said, twirling the curls in her hair like a little girl. She was wearing a light-blue dress with sequins on the bottom. It was the first time she appeared to be a lady.

I didn't say a word. "Carrie, I want to say I'm sorry for being over at your house."

Simon tried to interrupt her. "Now go on about your business, Nadine."

She sucked air in, and shook her head, then Nadine added, "You just don't want me to tell Carrie about yo sneaking ass, Simon." Afterward, she rolled her eyes.

"We don't want any trouble," I said, and waited for her to finish.

"I don't want Simon," she said and shot a cold eye at Simon. "We were just doing a little drinking and we lost control. I'm so glad you came home when you did. I'm so sorry," she said with as much drama as a vaudeville actor.

"Nadine, I'm trying to enjoy myself. I don't want to think about that day."

She seemed surprised by my reaction. "I didn't mean to cause no problems," she explained.

I saw the relief in Simon's face when she turned and walked back to a table across the room which she shared with a woman and two men — one of them, Jessie.

Everybody had come out for the event. It was Ms. Pearl's debut of her own songs. She finally had written something of her own. Everybody in the neighborhood appeared to be there. The lady next door, the corner store merchant, and the ice cream shop owner. There were more people there than ever before. The bartender was busy setting up drinks of Scotch and tap beer.

Simon got up and went to the bar for a Pepsi-Cola and peanuts. I looked around the room noticing many familiar faces from the community. The same lady who had made the comments to me earlier about Simon was sitting at the table with Nadine. It was then that I determined what they'd said about him had some truth. Now, he was attempting to prove to me that I was still his only love. I loved my husband even though he held secrets I thought could destroy our family. I supposed now I had some too.

"They say Ms. Pearl will be performing in a few minutes," Simon said.

"Where is she?"

"The bartender says she is here somewhere. She's probably in the back room."

"The back room . . ."

"Yeah!" He pointed to a door at the back of the room. A man was standing outside, guarding it like a soldier. "There are a lot of people here to keep order tonight."

"They need them after what happened the last time all these people were in here."

I took a sip of my drink. I thought how interesting it was that the entire community was out to hear Ms. Pearl perform her own songs. Her music was gaining a lot of fame, especially in Richmond, and the surrounding counties. There were even a couple of recognizable faces from Jefferson County.

Simon was rolled back in the chair with his arms around me, letting everybody know I was his wife. I saw Adam peering over at me, and when I decided to stare in his direction, he looked away.

Ms. Pearl walked up to the stage. She had on a form-fitting, ocean-green dress and stacked high heel shoes. Her face was heavily decorated with cinnamon powder and eyeliner. Her beautiful eyes seemed to sparkle. The crowd was clapping so hard, all other sounds were muted.

When she started to sing, the noise diminished. She had captivated the audience.

She bellowed out sounds accompanied by a pianist, a drummer, and a horn player. She was wailing her lungs out. Simon was feeling a groove and gazing at me. Everybody was enjoying her to the fullest. She appeared to be singing to somebody, but I couldn't tell who it was. After a while, I got up and excused myself to the bathroom in the back.

"You gonna be all right?" Simon asked me.

"I'll be okay. You can see the bathroom from here."

On the way there, I stopped by the table where Adam was sitting. The girl he was with was not there. "How are you, Adam?" I asked.

He looked up at me with those serious eyes. "I'm okay, but I miss you."

Before I could think things through, I answered, "I miss you too."

"If that's true, why are you with him?"

I was embarrassed by the question. I bent down to keep anyone from hearing. When I glanced over at the table where Simon and

I were sitting, he was watching everything I was doing.

"Can we talk later?"

"I'm available anytime," he said.

When I left, I could feel Adam watching me all the way to the bathroom, where two women were waiting in line. I got in line, and seemingly all eyes were on me. Along with Adam, Simon was also looking my way.

When I was coming out of the bathroom, I sensed somebody staring at me. I knew it was Adam. As I scooted through the crowd and the few women waiting in line on my way back to the table, somebody touched me on the shoulder. I turned to see who it was and nearly tripped to the floor. It was Herman Camm.

He smiled and asked me, "How is the baby?"

I was afraid to answer. I strutted quickly back to the table where Simon was sitting and bobbing his head to the sounds.

"What's wrong with you?" Simon asked.

"He's back," I said, shaking my head. "Herman Camm is still alive!"

"Why can't you let Herman die? He is not alive," he stated.

I inhaled deeply. "He is in here tonight. I saw him on my way to the bathroom."

He glanced around the room, searching

for Herman. After spotting Kindred, his brother, standing close to the bathroom, Simon paused before speaking, thinking how strikingly he resembled Herman. The fedora pulled down over one eye and the tailored suit were exactly the same. "If I didn't know any better, I'd think it was Herman my damn self," Simon mumbled, gazing at Kindred.

I didn't move. I kept an eye on the man. Simon pulled his chair close and put his arm around my shoulder. "Don't be scared," he said, "Herman is dead and gone. That cat is his brother."

Adam peered at me from across the room. The fear in my eyes was hard to ignore. While the music filled the air with jovial laughter, I couldn't help but wonder if Herman Camm would forever haunt me.

"But he asked about the baby, Simon."

"Well, Carrie, Robert is his nephew," Simon said.

I glanced at Adam, and he was still studying me as if he wanted to comfort me and hold me in his arms. The girl with him had returned to her seat and seemed unaware of his stares. I had every reason to talk to him now that Herman had also convinced my husband he was Kindred. Even though I was on a new path in Richmond, Virginia, I felt caught, fixed in time. The phantom of Jefferson County seemed to linger on.

ABOUT THE AUTHOR

Ruth P. Watson is the recipient of the Caversham Fellowship, an artist's and writer's residency in Kwa Zulu, Natal South Africa, where she published her first children's book in Zulu, *Our Secret Bond.* She has written for *Upscale,* the *Atlanta Journal-Constitution* and other publications. She is a documentary filmmaker, whose film, *I've Paid My Dues, Now What,* was aired on Public Broadcasting Channel. She was first-runner-up in the first-ever Frank Yerby Award. She is busy working on a film and book project. She is the author of *Blackberry Days of Summer.* She lives with her husband and son in Atlanta.